THE AFTER
SCHOOL
DETECTIVE
CLUB

THE
MYSTERY
IN THE MARSHES

Mark Dawson

WRITING WITH ALLAN BOROUGHS

ILLUSTRATED BY BEN MANTLE

WELBECK
FLAME

First published in 2023 by Welbeck Flame
An imprint of Welbeck Children's Limited,
Part of the Welbeck Publishing Group
Offices in: London – 20 Mortimer Street, London W1T 3JW &
Sydney – 205 Commonwealth Street, Surry Hills 2010
www.welbeckpublishing.com

Design and layout © Welbeck Children's Limited
Text © 2023 Unputdownable
Illustrations © 2023 Ben Mantle

A CIP catalogue record for this book is available from the British Library.

ISBN 978 1 80130 033 9

Printed and bound by CPI Group (UK)

10 9 8 7 6 5 4 3 2 1

To the girls of Godolphin School in Salisbury – thanks for the wonderful ideas on World Book Day.

Lucy

Brave, loyal and athletic. She wants to be

an Olympian so don't get in her way . . .

Max

The geek with a wicked sense of humour.

Self-styled child genius – just don't tell his mum.

Joe

Adventurous, funny and a great cook – but

don't believe everything he says.

Charlie

Fierce as a lion, she loves her dog Sherlock more

than people. Don't ever call her Charlotte!

Sherlock

Loud bark, cold nose,
big heart – the fifth
member of the club.

1

THE LETTER

Max Green stared in disbelief at the letter in his hands. He took a deep breath and forced himself to read the words again, his fingers trembling as their full meaning sank in.

Dear Maximillian, began the letter.

That was bad news for a start, thought Max. The only people who ever called him 'Maximillian' were his teachers and his mother, and it was rarely a good sign when they did.

This year, St Enid's School is participating in the prestigious Duke of Wellington challenge, which encourages young people to develop the essential skills they need to survive in the wilderness.

As one of our most academically gifted students, you are among those selected for the honour of participating in this rigorous outdoor assessment.

Max closed his eyes and shuddered. The words 'rigorous' and 'outdoor assessment' really had no business being in a letter addressed to him. He continued reading.

This year's challenge will take place in the beautiful Snape Marshes and the surrounding forests. All participants are expected to navigate their way on foot or by bicycle, spending no less than three nights under canvas and arriving at the final checkpoint by noon on the fourth day. You will be assessed on how well you perform your tasks with extra points awarded for demonstrating your survival skills and showing courage in the face of hardship. I do not need to tell you how important it is that our school does well in this exercise. I know that you will not let the school down.

2

The last line was underlined in red ink and the letter was signed by the headteacher. Max gulped and looked up. On the other side of the breakfast table, his father was looking at him eagerly.

'Well?' said his dad when Max had finished reading. 'What do you think? Isn't it wonderful?'

'Wonderful?' echoed Max. 'They're going to make me live out of doors for four days in the cold and the wet, *under canvas!* That means living in an actual tent, Dad. It's like something out of the Stone Age. How is that wonderful, exactly?'

Tony Green sighed. 'Now, don't be like that, Max,' he said, trying to keep the disappointment out of his voice and not entirely succeeding. 'When I was a boy, my friends and I were always off camping together in the summer months. It's the most fun a boy can have.'

Max put down the letter and held his head in his hands. 'The most fun a boy can have, Dad,' he said patiently, 'is spending the weekend in his bedroom with the new *Warlocks and Dragons* game, not sleeping in a field with a bunch of cows. Why have they picked me to go on this thing anyway?'

'It's like the headmaster said in his letter,' said his mother as she placed a plateful of toast on the kitchen table. 'They picked you because you are one of their best students.'

'Yeah. They picked you because you're such a geek!' The small girl sitting at the end of the table grinned gleefully at Max, showing off the gap in her front teeth.

'That is enough from you, Safiyah,' said their mother, raising a warning finger. 'Get on with your breakfast and don't annoy your brother.'

Max glared at his little sister. Even though she was only seven, Saffy always managed to be more irritating than a wasp at a picnic. When her mum wasn't looking, the little girl stuck her tongue out at Max before shovelling a spoonful of Frosty-Sparkles into her mouth and crunching noisily.

Max gave her a glare and turned back to his parents. 'Well, I can't go,' he said breezily. 'I mean, I know it's a great honour and everything. But there's a competition at the chess club on Saturday and I simply have to be there.'

'The competition can wait, Maximillian,' said his mother. 'Going on this adventure will be good for you and it will give you extra credit with the school, which means you'll get even better grades next year. Besides, I've already signed the papers to say you have permission to go, so we'll hear no more about it.'

'You've signed the papers?' Max slumped in his chair with the air of a condemned man. 'So, I really can't get out of it?'

'Cheer up, Max,' said his dad. 'This trip will make a man of you.'

'Yeah,' said Max. 'That's just what I'm afraid of.'

Joe Carter swept through his bedroom like a whirlwind, scooping up his phone, his front door keys and his sweatshirt before charging downstairs and heading for the front door.

'Er, Joe,' called his father from the kitchen. 'Before you go out, your mother and I would like a word with you.'

Joe paused with one hand on the front door. This did not sound good. He made a mental list of the things he might be about to get into trouble for.

There was the pet tarantula he had bought from a boy at school and was keeping in the bottom of his wardrobe, but he was pretty sure that no one knew about that yet. Perhaps it was the pot of ink he'd spilled in his bed three nights ago or the expensive cast-iron saucepan that he'd had to hide after a failed attempt to make toffee?

He was just thinking that the best thing to do would be to pretend he hadn't heard and slip out of the front door when his mother stepped into the hall. 'Oh no you don't,' said Penelope Carter. 'Come in here, at once.'

Joe hovered in the doorway of the kitchen like someone who might need to make a quick getaway. His mum and dad were sitting side by side at the far end of the table. 'Joe! Take a seat, buddy,' said his dad in a voice that was way too friendly for Joe's liking.

'What's this about?' he asked, sliding onto a chair.

His parents exchanged a glance. 'The thing is, Joe,' began his father in his most business-like voice. 'Penny, that is your mother, and I, have been doing some thinking about your future. We've made a difficult decision that took a lot of soul-searching. But it's one that I'm sure you'll agree is best for everyone.' He gave Joe a meaningful look. 'You do understand, don't you?'

Joe frowned. 'Er... you've made a difficult decision that will be best for everyone?' he repeated.

His father seemed immensely relieved. 'That's the spirit! You see, Penny, I knew the boy would understand.'

Joe shook his head. 'Er, no, I don't understand. What difficult decision?'

His father began to look uncomfortable again and shifted in his seat. 'Well, er, the thing is, your mother has decided. I mean, *we* have decided, that it would be best for all concerned if you... er... that is... er... if you...'

His mother rolled her eyes. 'Oh, for goodness' sake, Mike,' she snapped. 'We're sending you to boarding school, Joe. Now, it's all been arranged so let's not have one of your scenes. You're starting next term and that's all there is to it.'

Joe's eyes widened and his jaw dropped open. 'You're sending me away?' he gasped. 'To boarding school? B-but... which boarding school? Where is it?'

'St Grimshanks, in the Scottish Highlands!' said his father, cheering up again. 'It's a marvellous place, *very* exclusive. It was incredibly difficult to get you in but you're going to love it. They have five-mile cross-country runs every morning, cold showers, rigorous discipline and lights out at nine o'clock every night. It'll be the making of you, my boy!'

Joe's head began to feel all swimmy. Surely this wasn't happening. Surely he would wake up at any moment and discover he had been dreaming and that it was just a normal Saturday morning in Southwold. He squeezed his eyes tightly shut and shook his head. When he opened them again his parents were still looking at him.

'But I don't want to go,' he said. 'I want to stay here.'

'Well, I'm afraid that's not an option, Joe,' said his mother abruptly. 'I've been thinking for a while that it was about time I resumed my career. I've applied for a new job and if I'm successful then I won't be able to spend all my time taking care of you.'

Joe frowned. His mother's idea of 'taking care' of him mainly consisted of leaving him instructions for heating up frozen dinners. 'I don't need looking after,' he said. 'And I don't want to go to boarding school. I go to school right here in Southwold. All my friends are here.'

His parents exchanged another glance. 'Well, that's just the problem, isn't it, Joe?' said his mother. 'Ever since you started hanging around with these new friends of yours you've been getting into no end of trouble. First you stole the family motorboat to take them all joyriding and then there was that unpleasant episode when you took them to stay in someone else's castle without permission. And both times the police got involved, Joe. I was so ashamed I couldn't go to the golf club for a week.'

Joe thought of reminding his mother that they had used the motorboat to catch a gang of smugglers. And, when they had stayed at the castle, they had discovered a priceless Viking treasure. But he could tell that his mother was in no mood to listen to his arguments.

'You need to develop a better class of friends, Joe,' continued his mother. 'Lucy Yeung is always well presented, I suppose, even if her father is a bit rude. But that Max Green child is very peculiar, and as for that dreadful Charlotte Wells and her mangy little dog...' She shuddered visibly.

Joe looked down at the table. 'Charlie...' he mumbled. 'Her name's Charlie.' More than anything he wanted to be somewhere else right now.

'You'll make new friends, Joe,' said his mother, in a kindlier tone. 'People who'll be good connections for you later in life.'

Joe bit his lip. 'I don't want "good connections",' he muttered. 'I want my friends.'

'Don't sulk about it, Joe,' said his father. 'St Grimshanks will be a wonderful experience. You'll make us both very proud of you.'

Joe's fists came crashing down on the table. 'Why can't you just be proud of me now?' he shouted. 'All I want is to be with my friends. Why don't you want me to be happy?' He jumped up from the table and fled from the room before his parents could see him crying.

2

THE LAST BIG ADVENTURE

'Come on, you daft dog, jump! I know you can do it.' Charlie Wells stood in the centre of the beach hut, holding a doggy treat at arm's length above Sherlock's head. The little dog looked up at the piece of biscuit in her hand and a puzzled frown creased his forehead. Then he lay down on the floor and curled into a comfortable ball. He wasn't sure he understood this game at all.

'Give it up, Charlie,' said Lucy Yeung, who was lounging on the cushions in the corner. 'You've been trying to teach him that trick for days now. He's just not interested.'

'But I know he can do it,' insisted Charlie. 'He just needs the proper motivation, that's all.'

'Yes, he does,' agreed Lucy. 'But the trouble is, every time he doesn't do the trick you just give him the treat anyway. You're too soft on him; that's why he doesn't learn.'

Charlie made a face. 'I know, but I can't bear to not give it to him once he's seen it.' She sighed and sat down next to Lucy before tossing the

biscuit to Sherlock. Sherlock raised his head long enough to snap the morsel out of the air and then went back to sleep.

Just then, the door swung open and Max pushed his way inside. His hair was messy, and his usually immaculate tie was all twisted and creased. He was waving a crumpled letter in the air. 'Do you have any idea what they're going to make me do?' he spluttered. 'Well, *do* you?'

The two girls stared at Max uncomprehendingly. 'Nice to see you too, Max,' said Charlie. 'We're fine, thanks for asking.'

Max frowned. 'I'm sorry,' he said sulkily. He sat down at the table and helped himself to one of Sherlock's dog biscuits. 'It's just that they're going to make me go on this wretched Duke of Wellington challenge, which means that I'm going to have to travel across country for miles and miles, *without a car!* And as if that wasn't enough, they're going to make me sleep outside while I'm doing it. I mean, it's not the sort of thing a civilised person should have to do.'

Lucy laughed. 'Calm down, Max,' she said. 'The Duke of Wellington scheme is meant to make you challenge yourself and push your limits. It'll be good for you.'

'I challenge my limits every day,' said Max, taking another dog biscuit. 'How do you think I got to be a level ten Grand Wizard in *Warlocks and Dragons?*'

'I think the organisers were thinking of something that actually involved going outside,' said Charlie. 'Besides, camping is fun. Me and Sherlock do it in the summer. We cook all of our own meals and sometimes we walk for miles and miles without seeing another person.'

Max groaned and held his head in his hands. 'Why me?' he moaned softly.

'Don't be such a baby,' said Lucy. 'It's an honour to be asked to represent your school. I got my letter this morning too.'

'And me,' said Charlie. 'I meant to tell you earlier.'

Max looked up and blinked. 'You're both going too?'

'Sure,' said Lucy. 'I've been looking forward to it all year. We could all go together if you like?'

A look of relief passed across Max's face. 'That's brilliant, Luce,' he said. 'I mean, you're so much bigger and stronger than I am and—'

'I'm not carrying your stuff, Max,' said Lucy

firmly. 'So, forget it. We can go together but you still have to bring your own rucksack.'

The door opened again, and Joe stepped inside, looking even more furious than Max had done. 'Oh boy,' said Charlie. 'Everyone's in a cheerful mood today. What's the matter with you?'

Joe began to pace up and down the room in an agitated manner. His fists were clenched and his face was bright red. He seemed to be having trouble getting the words out. 'Boarding school!' he spluttered.

'What about it?' said Max.

'They're going to make me go,' cried Joe. 'Mum wants to get rid of me so she can go back to work and my dad thinks it will make a man of me. But I've looked at the website for St Grimshanks, and it's a terrible place. It looks like a prison camp.'

'You're not making a lot of sense, Joe,' said Lucy. 'Perhaps you should start at the beginning.'

She coaxed Joe to sit down while Charlie

boiled the kettle and made him a cup of tea. He told them all about the conversation with his mum and dad and the things he had found out about St Grimshanks. 'They only have boys in the school,' he complained. 'And they make you take cold showers and run cross-country in your shorts and vest, even in the winter. And...'. He paused for dramatic effect. *'They have lessons on Saturday mornings!'*

'But don't they know you've got friends here?' said Lucy.

'That's just it,' said Joe. 'They don't want me hanging around with you guys. They think you're a bad influence on me.'

'We're a bad influence on you?' cried Max, spluttering dog biscuit crumbs. 'After all the stunts you've pulled?'

Lucy frowned. 'That's terrible, Joe,' she said. 'When are they planning to send you?'

'Next term,' he said miserably. 'It means we've only got a few more weeks together and then

I'll be on my own again.' He looked so unhappy that they all felt very sorry for him and even Sherlock nudged up against his chair and licked his hand.

'I guess we won't be able to use this place either once you're gone,' said Charlie. 'It will be the end of the After-School Detective Club.' They all fell into gloomy silence as they pondered the prospect of no longer being able to meet in the beautiful beach hut they had been using as a clubhouse.

'Well, look on the bright side,' said Max eventually. 'At least you don't have to go on the Duke of Wellington expedition. We have to spend four days in Snape Marshes without getting drowned and then sleep in a field full of wild animals.'

Joe rolled his eyes. 'Oh, I know all about the Duke of Wellington,' he said. 'Apparently Grimshanks are very keen on open-air activities so my dad signed me up for the expedition to make them think I was the outdoors type. I'm going to have to come with you.' He slumped in his seat and buried his head in his hands.

'This is no good,' said Lucy. 'We have to do something to cheer ourselves up. If we've all got to go on the expedition, we should try and turn it into our last big adventure together. I was thinking of doing the cycling option. We could all take our bikes.'

Max stroked his chin thoughtfully. 'That might work,' he said. 'I've been working on something new that might be just the job for this trip.'

Joe grinned suddenly. 'Hey, you're both right,' he said. 'A cycling trip would be fun. I got a new mountain bike for Christmas and I've been dying to take it out for a proper ride.'

Max slapped Joe on the back. 'That's the spirit, Joe,' he said. 'I'm really glad you're coming along too. I mean, you're so much bigger and stronger than I am and—'

'Joe's not carrying your stuff either, Max,' said

21

Lucy. 'So, are we all agreed on taking our bikes?' Max and Joe nodded vigorously. 'What about you, Charlie? Are you up for it?'

Charlie had fallen silent and was staring down at the floor. Now she looked away from Lucy and shrugged. 'I'm not so sure,' she said. 'Sherlock and me are pretty busy over the next couple of weeks. I think I might skip the whole expedition thing.'

'Come on, Charlie,' said Joe. 'It's the last chance we'll get to spend some time together. What could be more important than that?'

Charlie turned on Joe with fire in her eyes. 'I already told you,' she snapped. 'I've got other things to do. Now get off my back and leave me alone.' She stood up suddenly. 'Come on, Sherlock,' she said. 'It's time we were going.'

Sherlock reluctantly got up off the mat and gave the others an apologetic look before following Charlie out of the door. As soon as the door slammed shut, the three friends looked at each other with puzzled expressions.

'What did we say?' said Lucy.

'Beats me,' said Max with a shrug. 'But you know Charlie, you can never tell what she's thinking.'

Then Joe slapped his forehead with the palm of his hand. 'I'm an idiot,' he gasped. 'I've just realised what's wrong with her. Charlie told me ages ago that she doesn't have a bicycle because her mum couldn't afford to buy her one. Then we started talking about taking our bikes on a cycling trip. That's why she won't come with us.'

'Oh no,' said Lucy. 'We all just planned to do something that Charlie can't join in with. I feel absolutely terrible. What are we going to do?'

3

WHAT FRIENDS DO

Brenda Wells sat cross-legged in the centre of her living room floor, wearing a pair of leggings and an old sweatshirt. Her eyes were closed, and her hands rested on her knees, the forefingers and thumbs touching to form little 'O's. On the floor in front of her, an incense stick burned in its holder while the sounds of whale song droned mournfully out of a speaker in the corner.

Charlie stood in the doorway and frowned at her mother. 'Mum?'

Brenda's chin drooped on her chest and Charlie could hear snoring above the sound of the whales. 'Mum!' shouted Charlie.

'W-what?' Brenda snorted and jumped. Her hands flew up in surprise, knocking over the incense and sending a cloud of fine ash into the air. 'W-what is it?' She blinked rapidly and then spotted Charlie in the doorway. 'Charlie, what are you doing there? Couldn't you see I was in deep meditation?'

'You were in deep sleep, Mum,' said Charlie. 'You were actually snoring this time.'

'Nonsense.' Brenda Wells scrambled to her feet and scooped up the incense ash from the carpet. 'I was on the verge of achieving oneness with the universe when you interrupted me. What do you want, anyway?'

'Where did you put Sherlock's dog food, Mum? You said you were going to get some when you went out earlier.'

Brenda frowned. 'Did I? Oh, sorry, darling, I forgot all about it. You can't expect me to remember things like that with everything I've got on my plate. Now, where did I put my sandals? I have to go into town and open up the shop. Miriam and the girls are coming in for a tarot reading later on.'

Charlie's mother ran a small shop near the pier, selling dusty crystals to tourists. The shop did very little business, but Brenda also ran a more profitable sideline, telling fortunes in the back of the shop every Tuesday and Thursday.

Charlie had once asked her mother why she didn't predict something useful, like next week's lottery numbers, but this had led to a huge row. After that they agreed never to discuss the topic of fortune-telling again.

Brenda gathered up her sandals and followed her daughter into the kitchen where Charlie was slamming cupboard doors and stacking dishes noisily in the sink. 'Honestly, darling, what *has* got into you? You've been crashing around the house all afternoon.'

'It's nothing, Mum,' said Charlie as she attacked a blackened saucepan with a scouring brush. 'I'm absolutely fine.'

'Well, you don't seem fine,' said Brenda. 'You're giving off waves of negative energy, darling. Besides, aren't you supposed to be getting ready for this Duke of Ellington thingy that you're going on with your friends?'

Charlie did not turn around but her shoulders

stiffened visibly. 'It's the Duke of Wellington,' she said in a tight voice, 'and I'm not going with them.'

A worried look came across Brenda's face. 'You aren't?' Brenda had always been aware how Charlie's bad temper stopped her from making friends. So she had been very pleased when Charlie had made friends with Lucy, Max and Joe, especially as they all seemed so polite. Brenda had secretly hoped that some of their good manners might rub off on her daughter. 'Well, why aren't you?'

'It doesn't matter, Mum. Just forget about it.' Charlie kept her back turned as she carried on with the washing-up, clanking the plates together furiously.

Brenda bit her lip. She assumed that Charlie must have fallen out with the others and felt a sudden urge to try and cheer her daughter up. 'Well, perhaps you and I could do something together while they're away?' she offered. 'Something we'd both enjoy.'

'There's nothing we'd both enjoy, Mum,' snapped Charlie. 'You and I have nothing in common.'

Brenda sighed. She would have liked to argue, but she knew that Charlie was absolutely right on this point. Brenda liked crystals and yoga and meditation while Charlie liked bird-watching, walking and dogs. They almost never did anything together. The thought made her feel suddenly sad. She decided to change tack. 'But *why* aren't you going away with your friends?' she said. 'Can't you just apologise and make it up with them?'

Charlie turned around with such fury in her eyes that Brenda took a startled step backwards. 'We haven't had an argument, Mum,' she yelled. 'I can't go because it's a cycling trip and I haven't got a stupid bike.' She went back to the washing-up with renewed violence.

Brenda blinked. 'Oh, I see.' At the mention of 'bikes', Brenda had been stung by a pang of guilt. Charlie had once asked her for a bike, on her seventh birthday. But Brenda had made very little money that year, and she simply couldn't afford it. When she had explained this to Charlie, the little girl had just clamped her mouth tight shut and had never mentioned bicycles again. Brenda had assumed that Charlie had forgotten all about wanting one.

'I didn't realise you still wanted a bicycle,' she said eventually.

'Forget it. It doesn't matter.' Charlie didn't turn around.

Brenda's expression brightened suddenly and she snapped her fingers. 'Wait a minute,' she said. 'We *have* got a bicycle you can use. Now that you're bigger you can use my old bike.'

Charlie turned and gave her mother a curious look. 'You haven't got a bike,' she said.

'Yes, I have. It's in the back of the shed; it would be perfect for you. I used it to cycle to Glastonbury Festival one summer with Miriam and the girls.'

'*You* cycled all the way to Glastonbury?'

'Well not exactly,' said Brenda. 'We cycled as far as the pier and then we caught the coach. But the point is, I put my bike in the shed afterwards and it's still there. It might need a bit of oil after all this time, but it should be fine.'

'After all this time?' repeated Charlie. 'How long ago was this, exactly?'

Brenda frowned thoughtfully. 'Let me see now, I think that must have been 1998.'

Charlie rolled her eyes. '1998! You're kidding me? That bike has been in our shed for over twenty years. It will be a pile of rust by now.' She pulled the plug out of the sink and let the water drain away while she wiped her hands on a tea towel. 'Just forget about it, Mum. Who wants to go on a rotten cycling trip anyway?'

An hour later, Charlie stood outside the garden shed wearing a thoughtful expression. Spread around the garden were the entire contents of the shed including a lawnmower that had rusted into an immovable block, a paddling pool with a hole in it, a tangled knot of hosepipe, a garden fork with bent prongs and about a thousand discarded plastic flowerpots. Underneath the old paddling pool, Charlie found what she had been searching for.

Leaning against the side of the shed was the oldest bike Charlie had ever seen. It was largely rust-brown with faint spots of pale green that gave a clue as to what colour it might once have been. The tyres were not only flat, but they seemed to have solidified in that shape so that no amount of air was ever going to make them round again. One of the brakes seemed to be immovably clamped around the front wheel and when Charlie tried to turn the pedals, the chain made a noise as though someone was massacring a lot of mice.

At least, thought Charlie, *it has a basket and a saddle.* Although when she looked inside the basket it looked like a family of rats had been living in it and the saddle had so many springs poking out that it looked like a medieval torture device for punishing witches.

She sat down heavily on the damp grass and held her head in her hands. This bike was never going anywhere, ever again. She had been kidding herself if she thought she could take it on an expedition with the others. She would just have to get used to the idea that she was not going.

At that moment, Sherlock sat up and barked and Charlie looked up to see Joe poking his head through the back gate. 'Am I interrupting anything?' he asked cheerfully.

'Yes,' said Charlie sullenly.

'Great,' said Joe, letting himself into the garden. 'Interrupting is one of the few things I'm good at.' He patted Sherlock and then caught sight of the bike leaning against the shed. Joe sucked his teeth noisily, the way he had seen the man at the garage do when his dad took his car in for repair. 'Wow, what a heap,' he said.

Charlie scowled. 'Tell me something I don't know,' she said. 'So, what do you want exactly? I'm busy.'

'I can see that,' said Joe. 'It's going to take a lot of work to get this pile of junk ready for the expedition next Saturday.'

Charlie got up and began angrily throwing items back into the shed. 'Did you just come here

to make fun of me, Joe?' she said as she hurled the garden fork like a spear. 'I know I can't go on the expedition so stop rubbing it in.'

'I'm not making fun of you,' said Joe earnestly. 'I came over to see if I could help.'

Charlie threw a bag of manure into the shed, which burst open and spilled across the floor. 'I don't need any help,' she growled.

Joe looked at the bike and scratched his chin. 'From the looks of this thing, I'd say you do,' he said. 'I could help you get it ready for Saturday.'

Charlie dragged the rusted lawnmower across the grass, making a large trench in the lawn. 'Forget it, Joe,' she said. 'You said it yourself, that bike is a heap. No one could ever get it going again.'

'I bet I could,' said Joe brightly. 'My dad's got loads of tools and spare parts for his mountain bike. We could take it over to my place and look at it in our garage.'

Charlie looked at Joe suspiciously, as though she was expecting a trick. 'You don't have to do that,' she said eventually.

'I know I don't,' said Joe. 'But I want to. It's what friends do, isn't it?'

Charlie stared at Joe for several seconds. 'I guess so,' she said with a shrug. Then she gave Joe an apologetic smile. 'I'm sorry I got angry. I'm not very good at having friends.'

Joe nodded in an understanding way. 'It's okay,' he said. 'Besides, there's another good reason for you and Sherlock to come over.'

'What's that?'

Joe grinned. 'My mum's going to hate it.'

4

PREPARATIONS

The sign on Max's bedroom door read *KEEP OUT:
Level 10 Grand Wizard at work (this means you,
Saffy).* Lucy read it and grinned, then rapped on
the wood.

'Get lost, Saffy,' came Max's voice from inside.

Lucy opened the door and peered in. At first,
she could see no sign of Max. His usually tidy
bedroom looked like the aftermath of an explosion
in a shop that sold camping equipment.

Distributed around the room were several small
saucepans, a camping stove, an inflatable mattress
(half-inflated) and a pair of brand-new walking
boots, still in their box. A large tent had been

unfolded and draped over the wardrobe and Max's bed was lost beneath piles of fleecy jumpers, thermal leggings and enough socks to supply a football team for a whole season.

'Max? Are you in here?'

Max's head popped up from behind the bed and he blinked at Lucy. 'Oh, it's you, Luce,' he said. 'Saffy keeps coming in here when I'm not looking and letting the air out of my inflatable pillow.'

Lucy wandered into the centre of the room and looked around with a bemused expression. 'Max, what *is* all this stuff?' she said. 'Did you rob a camping shop?'

Max stood up and adjusted his tie. 'Essential supplies, Luce,' he said. 'Things that the truly serious camper can't be without. I'm particularly proud of this.' He held up a device that looked like a fork with widely spaced prongs attached to a heavy handle. He pressed a button and the prongs began to pirouette around each other with a loud whirring noise.

'What is that thing?' said Lucy.

Max gave her a flash of his eyebrows. 'Electric marshmallow toaster,' he said proudly. 'For the complete campfire experience.'

'But why wouldn't you just use an ordinary fork?'

Max gave Lucy a disappointed look. 'Really, Luce, why would you want to use an ordinary fork when you have technology to do the job for you?'

Lucy did not answer. She was examining a pair of thick socks that had wires sticking out of them. 'Careful with those,' cried Max. 'Those are my battery-heated socks.'

'Are you serious?' Lucy held a battery-heated sock at arm's length.

'Keeping your feet warm is one of the most important things an explorer can do,' said Max earnestly. 'Once your feet get cold it's all downhill from there.'

'Max, we're only going away for four days,' said Lucy. 'Surely you don't need all this stuff?'

Max looked offended. 'How can you possibly

know what we'll need until we're actually out there in the wilderness?' he said. 'You'll be telling me I can't take my laptop next.'

'You can't take your laptop!' cried Lucy. 'The rules say we're only allowed to bring one phone between us in case of emergencies. Other than that, all you need are some warm clothes and a few spares in case they get wet. I don't even recognise half of this stuff. I mean, what is *this* meant to be?' She pointed to something draped across Max's bed that looked like a cross between a duvet and a spacesuit. It had a quilted hood and arms and a complicated series of zips and fasteners around the bottom.

'*That*,' said Max knowingly, 'is my *slee-backet.*'

'Your what?'

'It's a sleeping bag and a jacket combined,' explained Max. 'Watch.'

Lucy watched, as Max wriggled into the slee-backet. He pulled the bulky garment over his head and pushed his arms into the sleeves.

Then, with some considerable effort, he pulled the long, quilted skirt down to his shins. 'You see?' he said triumphantly. 'You wear it as a jacket during the day, then when you're ready to go to bed you just zip up the feet end and hey presto.' He grinned out of the quilted hood. 'How do I look?'

Lucy raised an eyebrow. 'You look like someone who came to a fancy-dress party as a caterpillar,' she said.

Poor Max looked so crestfallen that Lucy immediately regretted her words. 'Look, Max,' she said gently. 'Going on a camping trip is about getting back to nature. You should take as little as possible. There's far too much here for one person to carry. Trust me, you can leave at least half of this stuff behind.'

Max surveyed the mass of equipment and let out a sigh. 'I guess you're right, Luce,' he said with a shrug. 'I could thin it out a little. Just don't come crying to me when your wrist is aching from having to turn your own marshmallow fork.'

Lucy grinned. 'Okay, I promise. Come on, I'll help you to repack.'

They were interrupted by the sharp noise of a small stone pinging off Max's bedroom window, followed immediately by another, and then another. They grinned at each other. They had both become used to Joe's method of announcing his presence outside their bedroom windows.

Max flung up the window and they looked out. In the lane behind Max's bedroom, underneath a street lamp, were two people seated on bicycles. One of them was Joe, sitting astride his shiny new mountain bike. The other was Charlie.

Charlie was sitting on a tall bike with upright handlebars, a low crossbar and a sturdy chain guard. The whole bike had been painted in fresh green paint and there was a wicker basket mounted on the front. Best of all, Sherlock was sitting in the basket. He barked when he saw Max and Lucy.

'Charlie!' cried Lucy. 'You've got a bike!'

Even at a distance they could both tell that Charlie was beaming. 'I know, isn't it brilliant?' she said. 'It's my mum's bike really, but Joe helped me to fix it up. We rubbed off all the rust and repainted the frame. Then we repaired the punctures and oiled the chain. It's as good as new now. Well, it's a bit wobbly and the brakes squeak like anything but I still think it's the best bike in the world. Sherlock thinks so too.'

The little dog barked loudly, and they all dissolved into laughter. 'Oh, Charlie, that's fantastic. I'm so glad you're coming with us,' said Lucy. 'Joe, you're absolutely brilliant.'

Joe shrugged bashfully and then frowned.

'Max, what is that thing you're wearing, exactly?'

'Slee-backet,' said Lucy immediately. 'It's best not to ask. So, is everyone ready to leave on Saturday?'

Joe tore his gaze away from the slee-backet. 'Er, pretty much,' he said.

'Me too,' said Charlie. 'Mum dug out her old tent and rucksack for me. I'm going to pack just as soon as I get home.'

'So, it sounds like we're all set, then,' said Lucy. 'Who knows, we might even persuade Max that camping is fun.'

'I wouldn't bank on it,' muttered Max. 'Not unless hypothermia is on the list of things to do before you die.'

'Well, at least one thing's certain,' said Charlie. 'If we're going to be out in the marshes for four days, there's no chance we'll be having an adventure this time.'

5

GROUP CHAT

Max: Lucy?

Max: Luce, where are you? This is urgent.

Max: LUCY!

Lucy: Max, what is it? I was eating dinner. My phone's been going crazy.

Max: I need packing advice.

Lucy: Again? We already repacked your stuff, like five times!

Max: Which baseball cap should I bring? The one with the solar-operated fan or the one with the built-in Wi-Fi hotspot?

Lucy: How about neither. You'll need your cycling helmet and nothing else.

Max: Really?

Lucy: Yes, really. Just leave the other stuff behind. You'll have more space in your rucksack.

Max: You're right. That means I'll have more room for the hand-held weather station.

Lucy: Oh, brother.

Charlie: Hi. Jst fnshd pcking. Cnt wt 4 tmrw.

Max: Still using that prehistoric phone, I see, Charlie

Charlie: Thrs yrs of life lft in ths phne yet. Im svng th plnet by not gttng a new 1.

Max: Not much point being an eco-warrior if no one can understand anything you type. Besides, Lucy says we're only allowed one phone between us so bagsy we take mine. I don't think I could survive for four days with no technology at all.

Charlie: Fn by me

Lucy: And me.

Joe: Hi. Did I miss much? What's the plan for tomorrow?

Lucy: I've made us an itinerary.

Joe: Is that something we can eat with our fingers?

Lucy: It's a timetable, Joe. It says where we have to be on each day.

Max: Ideally, that would be a piece of paper with '*my bedroom*' written on it.

Lucy: I spent a lot of time working on this, so pay attention. We have to show our itinerary to Mr Finnegan tomorrow before we set off. After that he'll meet us at various points along the route to make sure we're ok. We have to get to the final checkpoint by midday on the fourth day or we'll all fail the expedition and have to redo it next year.

Max: Mr Finnegan the games teacher? That's not good. I don't think he likes me.

Lucy: Well, you're not exactly his star pupil are you, Max? Just try to look keen and I'm sure you'll be fine.

Charlie: Snds gd 2 me. Thks Lcy. Whr shll we mt tmrw?

Lucy: We have to check in with Mr Finnegan at 9 a.m. at the top of North Green. After that we can head down to Walberswick and pick up the cycle path from there.

Joe: I can't wait.

Charlie: Me nthr. C U thr

Lucy: How about you, Max? Aren't you excited?

Max: By the prospect of sleeping in the rain? Trust me, Luce, the most exciting thing that's going to happen to us in the next few days is having to wring out our socks. I guarantee this is going to be the dullest trip *ever*.

6

THE ROAD TO RENDLESHAM

The following morning, Joe was the first to arrive at North Green. While he waited, he tightened the straps on the saddlebags of his mountain bike and looked around at the scene.

The green was an ants' nest of activity. Some of the teachers from his school had set up a folding table on the grass and an excited cluster of children was gathered around it. All of them were laden with rucksacks and sported brand-new waterproof jackets.

While Joe was watching the scene, Lucy slid gracefully to a halt beside him on a sleek red racing bike with white handlebar tape and black panniers. 'Nice bike,' said Joe admiringly.

'Thanks,' said Lucy. 'My folks bought it for me last year when my dad had me training for a junior triathlon.' She checked her watch. 'I hope the others aren't late. We can't afford to miss our check-in time.'

'Here's Charlie now,' said Joe.

Charlie was coming up the hill on her heavy bike, standing upright on the pedals as Sherlock trotted along beside her. Her luggage was wrapped in an old tarpaulin, lashed to the back of the bike with a thick rope. When she arrived, Charlie was pink in the face and grinning broadly. 'We made it,' she gasped. 'It took me a while to get everything tied down but then getting here was really easy. I should have got this old bike out of the shed years ago.'

'Charlie, what *is* Sherlock wearing?' said Joe. The little dog was dressed in a black harness, strapped tightly across his shoulders. Two bulging pouches hung down either side of his body, fastened under his belly by another strap.

'I make him carry his own food,' said Charlie. 'Otherwise, he'll go through all of my luggage until he finds it. I strap it to his back because it's the only place he can't reach.'

Even as Charlie was talking, Sherlock was twisting his head around and trying to get a grip on one of the pouches with his teeth. Every time he turned towards it, the pouch would move a little further out of his reach so that he began turning in faster and faster circles on the footpath.

Lucy tapped on her watch. 'Where's Max got to?' she said impatiently. 'He knows what time we're supposed to leave. He'd better not have chickened out or I'll never let him hear the last of it.'

'I don't think he's chickened out,' said Joe. 'But you're going to wish he had. Look.'

Max was rolling up the hill towards them on his bicycle. He wore his usual fresh white shirt and tie together with the slee-backet, which flapped behind him in the breeze. He was sitting on a small bicycle with compact wheels, which appeared to be gliding up the hill without any effort on his part. When he drew alongside them, the bike came to a halt with a soft whine.

'What is *that* thing?' said Lucy.

'It's my electric bike,' said Max proudly. 'I made it out of spare parts from the battery-operated skateboard. Pretty neat, don't you think?'

'I think that's the coolest thing you've ever invented,' said Joe. 'Can I have a go? You can ride my mountain bike for a bit if you want?'

'Ride your bike?' Max curled his lip. 'Really, Joe, pedalling is *so* last year.'

'I'm not sure it counts as proper cycling,' said Charlie. 'I mean, you won't get any exercise riding that thing.'

'That, my dear Charlie,' said Max, 'is the whole point.'

Lucy looked aghast. 'But, Max,' she cried. 'They're never going to let you do the expedition on that thing. From what I hear, Mr Finnegan is a real stickler for the rules. I don't think he's going to like this one bit.'

'And what is it that I'm not going to like?'

They turned to see a skinny man standing behind them. He had lank, greasy hair that hung down the back of his head, even though he was quite bald on top, and he wore an ill-fitting, bright red polyester tracksuit with grubby white stripes along the arms and legs. His beady eyes darted to each of the children in turn.

'Oh, er hello, Mr Finnegan, sir,' said Lucy, flustered. 'We were just checking that we had all the right equipment with us. But it's all absolutely fine.' She smiled in what she hoped was a winning way and positioned herself in front of Max's bike.

Mr Finnegan would have made an excellent games teacher except for the fact that he hated physical exercise and children. There was nothing he liked better than to see a class of students getting cold and miserable as they ran around a muddy field, just as long as he didn't have to do it himself.

He looked the group up and down and his face settled into its customary scowl. 'As an officially licenced examiner for the Duke of Wellington awards,' he began, '*I* will be the one who decides whether you have the right equipment or not. Now stand back and let me get a proper look at your kit.'

The children all dismounted and stood next to their bikes while Mr Finnegan inspected each one in turn. He frowned at Charlie's ancient machine, but he could find nothing mechanically wrong with it. This seemed to make him even more irritated.

'What about phones?' he said sharply. 'You're only allowed one phone per group in case of emergencies, you know?'

'We know,' said Lucy. 'None of us have a phone except Max.'

Mr Finnegan looked like he was about to say something further when he caught sight of Max's bike. 'Good grief, Green!' he spluttered. 'Is that an *electric bike?*'

Max nodded proudly. 'Absolutely, sir,' he said. 'My own invention.'

Mr Finnegan stared. 'But that's against the rules.'

'Ah, well, that's where you're wrong, sir,' said Max earnestly. 'Last night I downloaded the Duke of Wellington rule book and I read the whole thing.

It doesn't say anything about electric bikes. Mind you I think the rules were written about fifty years ago, so I don't think electric bikes were invented then.'

Mr Finnegan blinked. He stared at Max, then at the bike, then he started to leaf through the sheaf of typed notes attached to his clipboard. There was a long and awkward silence while he ran a trembling finger along the page. When he looked up at the group, his face was purple.

'It appears, Green,' he said through gritted teeth, 'that you are correct. Unfortunately, I can find nothing in the rules that says you can't use an electric bike.' Max beamed with pleasure. 'But it just goes to prove what I've always said, Green. You are without doubt the laziest child in the entire school.'

'Thank you,' said Max. 'That's exactly what I keep trying to tell everyone.'

Mr Finnegan gripped his clipboard so tightly that his knuckles turned white and he began to quiver with rage. 'Enough of your cheek, Green,' he snapped. 'Where's your itinerary?'

Lucy fumbled in her pocket and held out a sheet of paper. Mr Finnegan snatched it from her hand and glowered at the neatly typed page. When he could find no fault with it, his scowl grew even deeper.

'Alright then,' he said eventually. 'I'll expect to see you all at the finishing line in four days' time. Keep to the paths and stay away from the airbase. I'll be checking up on you along the way.' His voice dropped to a threatening whisper. 'And if I find out that you've strayed off your planned route, I'll fail the lot of you.'

He shoved Lucy's itinerary into his pocket and then jabbed an accusing finger at Max. 'I'll be particularly watching out for you, Green,' he snarled. 'Put one foot out of line and I'll have you doing push-ups in the gym every day for a month. Now get going.'

He stalked away to begin shouting at another group of children on a different part of the green. 'Nice going, Max,' said Lucy with a frown. 'You've managed to tick off the one teacher who decides whether we pass or not.'

'Don't worry about him, Luce,' said Max. 'I've read that rule book from cover to cover. Finnegan will never be able to disqualify me.'

'Well, if you're quite done antagonising the judges,' said Charlie, 'shall we get a move on? It's nearly half past nine already.'

The four friends adjusted their cycle helmets and climbed onto their bikes. With Sherlock running alongside them, they set off down the road that led from the common to the harbour and rattled across the narrow bridge towards Walberswick.

The air was crisp, and the fresh wind rattled in the rigging cables of the sailboats in the harbour. They paused to look up at a flock of low-flying geese and shielded their eyes against the May sunshine reflecting off the flooded marshlands.

Before long they had left the town far behind and there was only the sound of the marsh birds and the wind and the soft whining of Max's electric bike as it crunched along the gravel path. 'Actually, this whole expedition thing isn't so bad,' said Max cheerfully, as he directed his electric bike up a small slope. 'I'm beginning to feel more rugged already.'

'Is it just me,' grunted Charlie, as she pedalled up the hill, 'or is everyone else hoping that his battery goes flat soon?'

It turned steadily warmer as the sun rose in the sky, and they had to stop to allow Max to remove the slee-backet, which he said was 'a bit like wearing a plastic bag, only less comfortable'. Charlie took the opportunity to give Sherlock a drink of water and then lifted him into her basket for a rest. When they moved off again, Sherlock put his paws up on the front of the basket and

his ears turned inside out in the fresh wind.

They were enjoying the ride so much that they completely lost track of time and everyone was surprised when Charlie called out from the back of the group, 'Hey, you guys. It's nearly 11.30; we've been going for two hours. How about we stop for a break?'

Max immediately veered off the path onto a stretch of grass. '11.30!' he exclaimed. 'Why didn't you say something sooner? That's pretty much lunchtime.'

They laid their bikes down by the side of the path and Lucy spread a plastic groundsheet across the damp grass. Max had brought a package of sandwiches from his mother, which looked large enough to feed an entire rugby team. 'There's cheese and pickle, sardines, egg salad and ham and tomato,' he said, laying them on the sheet. 'Help yourselves. There's plenty.'

'Blimey, Max,' said Joe. 'How long does your mum think you're going away for?'

'You can never bring too much food on an expedition into the wilderness,' said Max, clutching a sardine sandwich in one hand and an egg salad in the other and taking bites from both of them. 'Haven't you ever read the stories about people who ran out of food and had to resort to cannibalism?'

'There's no way I'm eating you,' said Joe. 'I've seen the things you eat when your mum's not looking. You probably contain more additives than a box of frosty-flakes.'

When the sandwiches had all gone, Joe pulled out a bag of chocolate brownies he had made himself while Lucy poured them all cups of hot tea from her flask. After they had completely stuffed themselves with food, they stretched out on the grass and soaked up the sunshine.

Charlie consulted her map and was delighted to discover that they had stopped next to a small nature reserve that was home to many wild birds. She pulled out her binoculars and spent the next half-hour lying on her stomach and peering out across the landscape. 'I have to say, Luce,' said Max, helping himself to another of Joe's brownies, 'this expedition isn't quite as awful as I was expecting.'

Lucy smiled. 'You wait until we get to the campsite I've picked out for us,' she said. 'That's when it will really start to get interesting.'

'Cycling is one thing,' said Max, 'but believe me, there is *nothing* interesting about camping in a forest.'

'Ah, that's not true,' said Joe. 'My dad told me loads of interesting things have happened in the forests around here. For instance, did you know that there was a famous UFO sighting near here?'

Lucy frowned. 'An unidentified flying object? Are you serious?'

Joe nodded eagerly. 'Sure. Apparently it landed somewhere near the US airbase and some people actually saw it on the ground. When they went back the next day to investigate, they found strange indentations in the mud left behind by its landing gear. I've seen the photographs.'

Max rolled his eyes. 'Good grief, Joe. What have I told you about believing everything you read on the internet?'

Joe frowned. 'It's true, I tell you. I've read all sorts of things about aliens and UFOs. Sometimes they even kidnap people and take them away in their spaceships. What's the matter, don't you believe in aliens?'

'Sure I believe in aliens,' said Max. 'What I don't believe is that aliens ever visit Southwold. I mean, why would they want to travel halfway across the galaxy to come here?'

Joe shrugged. 'I dunno. Maybe they like beaches?'

Charlie put down her binoculars. 'Max is right,' she said. 'There are billions of stars in the sky and there are probably millions of planets where aliens could live. The trouble is, they're all so far away from Earth that even if you could travel at the speed of light, it would take hundreds of years to get here.'

Joe's eyes widened. 'How come you know so much about it?' he said admiringly. 'I thought Max was the science geek?'

Charlie shrugged and held up her binoculars. 'Max isn't the only one who likes science,' she said. 'I like astronomy; it gives me something to look at when the birds have all gone to sleep. Trust me, the one thing we are definitely not going to see on this trip is aliens.'

7

LIGHTS IN THE MARSHES

They dozed in the sunshine for an hour until Lucy roused them and made them all get back on their bikes. 'We don't want to be late getting to the first campsite,' she said. 'If old Finnegan checks up on us and finds we're not there, he'll fail us instantly.'

It was hard to get going again; everyone was starting to feel tired and saddle-sore and even Sherlock curled up in the bottom of the basket and went to sleep. 'I envy you, Sherlock,' said Charlie, looking down at her sleeping dog. 'Lucy, are we nearly there yet?'

They had arrived at the edge of a broad

marshland with a brown river meandering through the middle of it. Lucy pointed towards a low hill, crowned with a thick wood of oak trees. 'That's Black Heath Wood,' she said. 'It's where we're going to camp tonight.'

'Thank goodness for that,' groaned Max. 'I've lost all sense of feeling in my bum.'

They followed the riverbank towards the trees, sending flocks of wading birds scuttling away across the mud. 'Look,' cried Charlie excitedly, pointing at some long-billed birds. 'Those are godwits and over there, that's a sandpiper. The marshes are really important for wildlife. Did you know there are otters living here, and even adders?'

'Adders?' said Max, alarmed. 'You mean actual snakes? Honestly, Charlie, why did you feel the need to tell me that? I'll never get to sleep now.'

The path veered away from the river and took them up the hill and into the forest. They followed the track until they reached a wide clearing that provided a view through the trees to the marshlands below.

'Wow, brilliant view, Lucy,' said Joe, climbing down off his bike. 'This place is so quiet. It's like no one ever came here before.'

'It's great, isn't it?' said Lucy. 'The trees should shelter our tents and there's a lake over there where we can get water for washing and cooking.'

'We should pitch our tents in a semi-circle and then light a campfire in the middle,' said Joe. 'I brought some marshmallows we can toast. They're vegetarian ones, especially for Charlie.'

'Lucky I brought my electric marshmallow toasting fork with me,' said Max. 'It's absolutely the last word in modern campfire conveniences.' He grinned as he saw Lucy rolling her eyes.

They leaned their bikes against a tree and started to put up their tents while Sherlock inspected all the trees for interesting smells. Lucy was the first to complete the task, assembling her tent in record time. Joe finished soon after, although his tent looked a little saggier than Lucy's.

Charlie had borrowed her mum's old army-surplus tent, which was made of green canvas with wooden tent poles. It took a long time to put it up but, when she had finished, it was by far the largest and most comfortable-looking of the three.

Meanwhile, Max laid out the pieces of his brand-new tent on the ground. He studied the instructions for a long time before crawling into the loose tent and attempting to assemble the tent poles from the inside. After several minutes he had become tightly wrapped in several yards of nylon sheeting and was wriggling around on the forest floor like an overgrown grub.

'You okay in there, Max?' said Lucy. 'Do you need any help?'

The overgrown grub went still. 'I'm fine, thanks,' came Max's muffled voice. 'It's quite comfortable in here, really – in fact, I think I'm just going to turn in early.' There was a brief pause. 'Although I kind of wish I'd gone to the bathroom first.'

The others grinned and set about unwinding Max. Joe helped him to assemble the tent properly while Lucy set about digging a small fire pit in the soft earth and Charlie and Sherlock went to look for firewood. In less than half an hour, as the evening gloom settled on the camp, they had a crackling fire.

Joe unpacked his camping stove and got busy with his frying pan and very soon the air was filled with the delicious smells of sausages. Joe handed around plates of sausages and beans and then cut up two extra sausages for Sherlock, which the little dog wolfed down hungrily.

After dinner they stacked the plates in a neat pile. 'We can wash them in the morning when we go down to the lake,' said Lucy. 'Now, Joe, how about those marshmallows?' Joe produced a large bag of the pink and white, squashy treats, which they skewered on long sticks and held out in front of the fire.

Max's electric marshmallow toaster proved to be something of a disappointment. Each time Max switched it on, the rapid rotation of the fork would fling the marshmallows across the camp, whereupon Sherlock would snap them out of the air and wolf them down in one bite.

'Face facts, Max,' said Lucy with a giggle. 'Your electric toasting fork is useless.'

'There is absolutely nothing wrong with my toasting fork,' said Max with a sniff. 'I think it's these marshmallows that are faulty.' But he still took the stick that Lucy offered him and toasted his marshmallow the same way as everyone else.

When they had finished eating, they brushed their teeth with water from their drinking bottles then got into their sleeping bags, lying with their heads out of the tents as they watched the dying embers of the fire. 'That was the best day,' said Joe with a yawn. 'I can't imagine

I'm going to be having any fun like this after I go to St Grimshanks.'

'Perhaps we could send you food parcels or something?' said Max. 'You know, like when prisoners get stuff sent from home.'

'Not helping, Max,' said Joe glumly.

'Try not to think about it too much,' said Lucy. 'Let's just enjoy the time we have left together.' She clicked on her torch to examine her map. 'I've already planned the agenda for tomorrow. After breakfast, we'll cross the river at the bridge and then it's just a couple of hours until we get to the forest.'

'You mean the forest with the aliens?' said Joe.

'Don't hold your breath for aliens,' said Max. 'I think the most alien thing we're going to see tomorrow is one of Finnegan's dreadful tracksuits.'

'Sherlock, for goodness' sake!' cried out Charlie in the darkness. 'He's wriggled down inside my sleeping bag and gone to sleep. Can you believe this dog?'

'I think he's got the right idea,' said Joe, with another yawn. 'I'm going to get some kip. Night all.' And with that he retreated inside his tent and pulled down the zip.

As they settled down for the night, Max called out in the darkness. 'Hey, guys,' he hissed. 'I was serious when I said I needed to go to the bathroom. Where am I meant to go and... you know?'

Lucy laughed. 'Oh boy, you really don't know anything about camping, do you?' she said. 'Here, take these.'

She tossed something to him, which clanked onto the ground in front of Max's tent. He clicked on his torch and saw a roll of toilet paper and the trowel that Lucy had used to dig the fire pit. He stared at the items for several seconds with a puzzled expression. 'What am I meant to do with these?' he said.

Charlie giggled while Lucy explained patiently exactly what Max was meant to do with the trowel. Max's eyes widened in horror. 'Are you serious! How uncivilised can this trip get?'

He unzipped the bottom of his slee-backet and hitched it up around his waist before scrambling out of the tent. Then he shambled off into the woods, complaining how expeditions should only be allowed to go to places with proper bathrooms. Charlie was now laughing uncontrollably in the darkness.

'I never knew anyone who was so out of place on a campsite,' she snorted. 'Do you suppose he'll be alright on his own?'

Lucy giggled. 'If he needs anything, I'm sure he'll let us know,' she said. 'Besides, how much harm can he come to out there?'

'I guess you're right,' said Charlie with a yawn. 'I'll see you in the morning.'

'Yeah, see you.'

They both withdrew into their tents and Lucy snuggled down in her sleeping bag. *Maybe I should check that Max is alright*, she thought sleepily as she closed her eyes. But she was too tired to act on the thought and a few moments later she was sleeping peacefully.

Meanwhile, Max was swearing under his breath and wrinkling his nose as he shovelled earth back into the hole he had dug a few minutes earlier. He stamped it down with his foot and gave it a last glare before turning away. *Camping is so undignified*, he thought.

He looked around for a place to wash his hands and shivered. It was dark away from the campfire, and his torch barely penetrated the thick tangle of branches for more than a few feet. It was then that he spotted a watery gleam coming through the branches.

When he pushed his way through the undergrowth, he found a small clearing with a wide pool lying still and silvery in the moonlight. On the far side of the clearing, the trees had been cut back and gave an uninterrupted view across the marshes to the other side of the river.

There was a hazy moon behind the clouds but there were no other lights at all.

Max crouched down to wash his hands and splash a little cold water on his face. When he looked up, he noticed a light on the far side of the marshes that had not been there before. It did not seem to come from a torch; it was too bright and fast-moving for that. There was no sound, but the eerie light moved swiftly back and forth across the mudflats, changing direction rapidly as though it was searching for something.

Max held his breath and his heart thumped inside his chest. With a shiver, he remembered their conversation at lunch and a single word popped into his head.

Aliens!

He had a sudden urge to run back through the trees to the safety and warmth of the campsite, but his legs seemed determined to stay rooted to the spot. Then the light stopped moving suddenly, hovering motionless in the sky,

almost as if it had become aware that someone was watching it. Max stood transfixed, scarcely daring to breathe until, very slowly, the light began to move across the river towards him.

He dropped the trowel and the toilet roll and turned to flee through the forest. Somewhere along the way he dropped his torch and blundered blindly through the branches, shrieking at the top of his voice.

'Help! Somebody! They're coming for me,' he cried. 'Don't let them take me.'

He crashed through a particularly thick tangle of branches and tripped headlong onto the soft earth. When he looked up, there were more lights coming through the trees towards him. 'No, please!' he gasped. 'Don't take me back to your planet!'

'Max what are you shouting about?' said Lucy as she crouched down next to him. 'Are you alright?

Max blinked up at Lucy and at Joe and Charlie, who were standing behind her, holding their torches. 'A-a-a-aliens!' he blurted.

'Oh boy, he's really lost it this time,' said Charlie.

'It's true, honestly,' gasped Max. 'I just saw a UFO.'

'You actually saw a UFO?' said Joe, his eyes suddenly wide with delight. 'Where was it?'

'Back there,' said Max, pointing back through the trees. 'Flying backwards and forwards over the marshes. I think they were coming to get me.'

'Max, there's no such thing as UFOs,' said Lucy patiently. 'You probably just saw the moon.'

Max stood up and brushed the mud from his slee-backet with as much dignity as he could muster. 'I was *not* looking at the moon,' he said sternly. 'Come and see if you don't believe me.'

They trooped back through the trees to the edge of the pool and looked out across the marshes. But there was nothing to see except a flat expanse of mud and reeds, grey and monochrome under the moon.

'It was right here,' insisted Max. 'I saw it flying around. And then it came this way.'

'Perhaps they activated their cloaking device?' said Joe helpfully.

'We're not encouraging this, Joe,' said Lucy.

'If there had been anything here,' said Charlie, 'Sherlock would have noticed it before now.' At the mention of his name, Sherlock 'ruffed' as though to confirm that he would have definitely noticed if there were any aliens in the vicinity.

'I'm sure there's a perfectly simple explanation,' said Lucy. 'But I'm too tired to think what it might be right now. I say we go back to bed and think about it in the morning.'

Max's shoulders drooped as they started back to the camp. He had been so sure he had seen something, but now he just felt like a fool. He took one last look across the marshes before following his friends.

8

BYRON J. HECKLEGRUBER

The following morning, Lucy stuck her head out of her tent and inhaled a deep lungful of the fresh morning air. The sun had broken through the early mist and filled the little clearing with golden light, even though it was still crisp and cold.

When she looked around, she was surprised to find Max, huddled next to the embers of the campfire, still wrapped in his slee-backet. 'Morning, Max,' she called cheerfully. 'You're up very early.'

Max scowled. 'Strictly speaking,' he said, 'I'm up

very late. I couldn't get to sleep for ages last night. Then I discovered we'd put my tent on top of a giant rock that was digging into my kidneys. And as if that wasn't enough, the tent was full of man-eating gnats. I've been bitten half to death.'

Lucy stretched her limbs. 'You're supposed to do up the flaps when you leave the tent,' she said. 'Don't worry, I've got some antiseptic in my saddlebag; I'll go and get it for you.'

As Lucy headed off towards her bicycle, Joe appeared from his tent, clutching a small frying pan and a box of eggs. 'Morning, all!' he said cheerfully. 'Who wants a fried-egg sandwich?'

While Joe lit the camping stove and cracked the eggs, Charlie emerged from her tent and Sherlock began his morning inspection of the camp.

A few minutes later, they saw Lucy returning with a worried expression. 'What's up, Luce?' said Charlie.

'My bike's got a slow puncture,' said Lucy. 'I've pumped it up again, but I'll need to repair it before we go much further. I've got a spare inner tube, but I didn't bring any tools.'

'Perhaps we could borrow some at the next village we come to,' said Charlie.

They agreed that as soon as they had had eaten, they would pack up the camp and find a place to repair Lucy's bike. They wolfed down Joe's fried-egg sandwiches while Lucy made some fresh tea for her flask and Charlie fed Sherlock some of the food from his doggy backpack.

After breakfast, they took the dirty plates down to the pool to wash them but as they drew nearer, Sherlock raced ahead through the trees, barking madly. 'What's got into him?' said Charlie.

As they reached the pool, they discovered the reason for Sherlock's behaviour. Lying on the ground was a shiny mountain bike, and, sitting beside it on a log, was a young boy.

He was about their age, with reddish-blonde hair, round glasses and a pale face with a smattering of freckles. He was preoccupied with Sherlock, who was sitting obediently and allowing the boy to tickle him behind the ears, the way that Charlie did. The little dog was clearly enjoying himself.

Charlie's eyes narrowed when she saw a stranger petting her dog. 'Sherlock!' she snapped. 'Come over here.'

Sherlock gave her a guilty look then glanced apologetically at the boy before slinking back to where Charlie was standing. The boy stood up and frowned.

'Is this your dog?' he said. He had a strong American accent. 'Found him wandering around; I thought he was a stray.' He looked at Charlie disapprovingly as he said this.

Charlie's eyebrows knitted together in a scowl, which the others recognised as an early warning sign. 'My dog is not a stray,' she said in a tight voice. 'And I don't like anyone I don't know touching him.'

The boy sniffed and looked down his nose. 'Well, in that case,' he said, 'why isn't he on a lead?

Don't you Brits ever train your dogs properly? Stray dogs are a menace.'

Charlie's face turned red and the others looked at each other uncomfortably. They all knew that the quickest way to end up in Charlie's bad books was to criticise Sherlock. 'My dog is *not* a menace!' she said, doing her best to control her temper.

'He's very well behaved. Besides, what do *you* know about training dogs?'

The boy gave an irritating smirk. 'I know plenty,' he said. 'Back home we used to have a whole pack of 'em. I reckon I know everything there is to know about training dogs. I could train yours for you if you like?'

Charlie's face went from red to purple and Lucy intervened hastily. 'My name's Lucy,' she said, giving the boy a friendly smile. 'And this is Joe, Max and Charlie. And that's Sherlock.'

The boy looked at the others as if he was noticing them for the first time. 'My name is Byron J. Hecklegruber the third,' he said with a sniff. 'So how about you tell me what you're all doing in *my* forest.'

'This isn't your forest,' said Charlie, still looking like she could cheerfully strangle him. 'Anyone's allowed to camp here.'

'That's where you're wrong,' said the boy. 'My dad rents the big house on the other side of the river.' He pointed through the trees. 'And all the land around here belongs to the house, so technically, you're in *my* forest.' He folded his arms triumphantly.

Lucy drew a deep breath. 'Well, we're very sorry that we camped in *your* forest,' she said. 'We'll be gone as soon as we've packed away our things.'

The boy shrugged. 'That's okay,' he said with a generous wave of his hand. 'You have my permission to stay as long as you want.'

Lucy rolled her eyes and crouched down beside the pool to fill her water bottle. She was usually very good with people, but this boy was one of the rudest individuals she had ever met.

Byron J. Hecklegruber watched while they brushed their teeth and washed the dishes. 'So, where y'all from?' he demanded after a while. 'Me and my dad are from California. That's in the US of A, if you didn't know.'

'I went to California on holiday once,' said Joe

brightly. He seemed genuinely interested in the boy. 'It's a great place.'

Byron J. Hecklegruber seemed pleased by this. 'It sure is,' he said proudly. He looked around. 'Best place in the world. It sure beats this dump, anyhow.'

'Is your name really Byron J. Hecklegruber the third?' asked Max. 'That's quite a lot of names.'

The boy's smile widened. 'You bet,' he said. 'I come from a long line of Hecklegrubers. There's so many of us that we need numbers as well as names.'

Lucy finished filling her water bottle and stood up. 'So are your family here on holiday?' she said.

Byron shook his head. 'No, we're here because of my dad's job. He's a colonel at the US Air Force base. He's a test pilot. He flies fighter jets.'

Joe's eyes grew as round as saucers. 'Fighter jets!' he gasped. 'That sounds like the coolest job ever! Does he ever let you fly them?'

Byron frowned. 'Boy, you're really dumb,' he

said. 'You need years of training before they let you fly a fighter jet.'

'My dad's taking flying lessons,' said Joe, undaunted. 'Just small planes, not jet fighters. He lets me go along and watch sometimes but he won't let me have a go.'

'Well, I'm sure the people of Suffolk will be very glad to learn that, Joe,' said Max. He turned to Byron. 'Perhaps you can help us? One of our bikes has a puncture. Do you know somewhere we could borrow some tools?'

Byron looked thoughtful for a moment. 'I guess you could come to our place,' he offered. 'We've got a whole outhouse full of tools. You could stay for a while too, if you like?' he added.

Charlie scowled. 'No thanks,' she said. 'We're in a hurry.'

'What Charlie means,' said Lucy quickly, 'is that we don't have a lot of time to spare. But it would really help if we could borrow your tools. Are you sure your dad won't mind?'

Byron gave a dry laugh. 'He won't care,' he said. 'Dad's always so busy at work that he's hardly ever home.' He turned and pointed along the river. 'We'll have to cross at the bridge to get to my house.'

'That's great,' said Joe. 'We were going that way anyway. We're going to camp in the forest tonight.'

'OK, cool,' said Byron. 'Why don't you get packed up and then we can head out.' He seemed to be less rude now that they had agreed to go to his house. Lucy wondered if he had many visitors.

They returned to the camp and quickly packed away their sleeping bags and tents. Max's tent had become such a tangle that he simply rolled it into a giant ball and lashed it to the back of his bike with the guy ropes.

When Byron saw Charlie's bike, he laughed out loud. 'Oh boy,' he cried. 'That's got to be the oldest bike I ever saw. Where did you get that clunker from?' Charlie fumed silently and gave Byron one of her most dangerous looks, though the boy didn't seem to notice.

What made things worse for Charlie was that Sherlock really seemed to have taken a liking to the boy. He followed him around the camp while they were packing and, when they set off on their bikes, he insisted on running alongside Byron's mountain bike at the front of the group.

Charlie pedalled along at the back, next to Lucy. 'I hate him,' she growled. 'I swear, if he's rude to me again, I'm just going to let Sherlock bite him.'

'Don't be too hard on him,' said Lucy. 'He's probably just lonely. Besides, Sherlock really seems to like him, and you always say he's a good judge of character.'

Charlie rolled her eyes. 'Well, Sherlock seems to have got it wrong this time,' she said.

They followed a winding trail that ran beside the river. Beyond the reeds, a large expanse of flat mud extended all the way to the opposite bank, with just a narrow ribbon of water meandering through the middle.

'The river doesn't look very wide here,' said Joe as they cycled. 'It looks like you could just walk across the mud.'

Byron laughed. 'That's a good way to get yourself killed,' he said. 'Them mudflats might look harmless, but my dad says you can sink in 'em real quick if you ain't careful.'

They crossed the river by a small bridge in a village that was little more than a few houses and some closed shops. They stopped briefly so that Lucy could pump up her tyre, which had gone flat again.

'My dad and me come here to buy groceries sometimes,' said Byron. 'It's pretty much the only time we ever see anyone else.'

'Don't you have any other family?' said Lucy.

'No,' said Byron. 'I don't have brothers or sisters and my mom died when I was just little. Since then, it's just been me and my dad.'

'What about school?' said Lucy. 'Don't you have friends there?'

Byron shrugged. 'My dad don't want me going to a regular school,' he said. 'He gets real worried about security because of his job. I have a tutor at the house three times a week, but I usually skip out of lessons when I can.' He laughed. 'Dad got real angry about that when he found out. He said next year, he's going to send me to a military academy.'

'What's a military academy?' said Joe.

Byron snorted. 'It's a school where they train you for a job in the army or the air force. They have very strict discipline there. You have to salute the teachers and they make you get up early to do hard exercise.'

Joe nodded sympathetically. 'It sounds just like St Grimshanks,' he said. 'I know how you feel.'

'Dad says it'll be "character-building", whatever that means.' Byron made a face to show just what he thought of that idea.

Then his expression brightened. 'Hey, maybe I should come camping with you guys for a few days? I used to camp out all the time when we lived in California. I could show you Brits how it's done properly. You could learn a lot from me. What d'you say?'

The four friends exchanged glances. When Byron wasn't being rude, he seemed to be extremely boastful and none of them really wanted to spend more time with him than they had to.

'We don't need anyone to "show us how it's done",' growled Charlie. 'We do just fine by ourselves, thank you.'

'What Charlie means,' said Lucy hastily, 'is that I'm not sure we're allowed to bring you along. The rules of the expedition are pretty strict.'

Byron's face fell. He dug his hands in his pockets and stuck out his bottom lip. Then he shrugged as though it was totally unimportant to him. 'OK, it's your loss,' he said. 'I got better things to do anyway.'

Lucy finished pumping up her tyre and they continued on towards Byron's house. It was slow going because Max's batteries were beginning to run flat and he was struggling to get up the hills. But after another couple of miles, they came over a low rise and saw the house on a wide, grassy slope, facing the river.

'Wow,' said Max. 'That's some place you've got there.'

The house was a large Tudor mansion, made of red brick with a tile roof and narrow chimneys. Green ivy grew up the walls and the house stood in well-kept grounds with neatly manicured lawns and mature trees. A high wall enclosed three sides of the property and the river ran along the fourth side at the bottom of the garden.

'It *is* pretty cool,' said Byron, evidently pleased.

'Your house is bigger than our whole school,' said Joe. 'Do you and your dad live there by yourselves?'

'Pretty much,' said Byron. 'We've got a gardener and a housekeeper. But that's about it. Most of the time I'm just there on my own. I can pretty much do whatever I want.'

They continued on to the house until they reached a set of black, wrought-iron gates set into the wall. Byron took a remote control from his pocket and pressed a button that made the gates swing open soundlessly. Then they followed him up the long gravel drive towards the house.

There were several outbuildings around the outskirts of the property and a rickety swimming platform tied up down by the river. Byron led them to a brick outbuilding with green-painted doors.

'This is where we keep the tools,' he said. He led them into a well-kept storage room filled with gardening equipment, oil cans and sacks of fertiliser. Along one wall, racks of well-oiled tools hung in their allotted spaces above a tidy work bench.

'You'll find what you need in here,' said the boy. 'Just make sure you put everything back. My dad hates people touching his stuff.'

Lucy leaned her bike against the wall and then looked along the rack until she found what she was looking for. 'An adjustable spanner and a set of tyre levers,' she said. 'That's perfect. It shouldn't take me more than twenty minutes to put the new inner tube in.'

As Lucy rolled up her sleeves and set to work, Byron beckoned to the others. 'Come and have a look around,' he said. 'I'll give you the grand tour.'

Leaving Lucy behind, Byron showed them the grounds, which included an orchard and a greenhouse where they grew herbs and tomatoes. Then he led them across the close-cropped lawn towards the front door.

'Wait until you see the old place,' he said excitedly. 'It's full of all kinds of secret hiding places. There's even a hidden chamber behind the wall in my bedroom. They say parts of the house are nearly five hundred years old.'

'Twice as old as America,' said Max thoughtfully. 'Imagine that!'

Charlie and Joe sniggered but Byron did not seem to notice the joke. All of his former rudeness was gone now, and he seemed delighted to have the opportunity to show off to someone.

As they approached the front entrance, the big oak door swung open and a severe-looking woman stepped out onto the front porch. She narrowed her eyes as they drew near. 'That's Mrs Bukowski,' said Byron, under his breath. 'Our regular housekeeper is off sick, so the agency sent her instead. She's a little bit scary but don't worry, I can handle her.'

Mrs Bukowski was more than just a little bit scary. She watched them with eyes that were so cold and so hard that Charlie, Joe and Max all dropped back, while Sherlock gave a little whine and kept close to Charlie's legs.

'You did not inform me that you had invited guests this afternoon, Master Byron,' she said as they drew near. She spoke with a clipped accent.

'Oh, they aren't staying long,' said Byron airily. 'I'm just going to show them the house while they're here.'

He tried to move past her, but Mrs Bukowski blocked his way. She raised one eyebrow a quarter of an inch, and the effect was terrifying. 'I'm afraid that is quite impossible, Master Byron,' she said firmly. 'I have just cleaned the floors and I cannot have muddy pawprints all over the house.' She looked disapprovingly at Sherlock as she said this.

Byron swallowed. 'I wanted to show them my bedroom,' he said in a slightly smaller voice. 'Couldn't we just—'

'No, you cannot!' Mrs Bukowski's reply was like an axe being brought down on the conversation. She glared at Byron for several seconds, as though daring him to answer back. Then she smiled, a tight smile that didn't quite reach her eyes. It was the smile of a viper.

'Your father will be home soon,' she said. 'I think your friends should go now.' She crossed her arms in a way that made it clear that the conversation was over.

For the first time, Byron's confident expression faded. It was very clear to the others that he was frightened of the woman. 'Alright,' he mumbled. He turned to the others and jerked his head. 'Come on, we'd better do as she says.'

They walked away from the house, watched closely by Mrs Bukowski. When Charlie glanced back, she saw the woman was still wearing the snake-like smile.

'What a horrible woman,' said Joe as soon as they were out of earshot. 'How do you put up with her?'

Byron looked angry and embarrassed after his encounter with Mrs Bukowski. His brows were knitted together, and his face was flushed bright red. 'I hate her,' he spat. 'I'm going to talk to my dad and get her fired just as soon as he gets home. You see if I don't.'

The others looked at each other awkwardly, not quite knowing what to say. They were glad when there was a shout from the direction of the tool shed and they saw Lucy standing outside with her bike.

'Well, it looks like Lucy's all done,' said Max. 'Perhaps we'd better go. I'd hate to get you into any more trouble.'

They returned to the tool shed and collected their bikes, then Byron walked with them down the drive towards the metal gates. 'Well, thanks for your help, Byron,' said Max, holding out his hand.

Byron seemed to have forgotten all about his earlier embarrassment. 'No problem,' he said. 'It's a good job I was here to help you out. If you ever need any advice on camping, just give me a call.'

Charlie looked ready to tell Byron exactly what she thought of his advice, but at that moment, the iron gates swung open and a large black car turned in to the drive. They all stepped aside as the car pulled up and the driver's window slid down noiselessly.

The man driving the car had iron-grey hair, styled in a short bristle cut. His eyes were steel-blue and his face looked like it had been chiselled out of granite. He was wearing a well-pressed blue uniform with a silver eagle on each epaulette.

This could only be Byron's father, the air force colonel.

He regarded the children fiercely. 'Byron, who are these people?' he demanded.

For the first time, Byron seemed truly flustered. He licked his lips and gulped. 'T-they're just friends, Dad,' he stammered. 'Lucy had to fix her bike and I said they could come and use our tools and then—'

'Silence!' The colonel's voice sounded like he was used to giving orders and having them obeyed. Byron stopped talking immediately. 'How many times have I told you, you are *not* to bring strangers to our house without my permission?' said the colonel. 'It's a security risk.'

Byron looked down at his feet. 'I'm sorry, Dad,' he mumbled.

'We're very sorry too, Colonel, sir,' said Lucy, stepping forward bravely. 'It's just that I had a puncture and Byron kindly agreed to let us—'

The colonel turned his cold gaze on Lucy.

'When I need an answer from you, young lady, I will ask for it,' he barked. 'Byron, please get in the car.'

Poor Byron looked thoroughly humiliated, but he did as he was told and walked around the car to get in the passenger door. He gave them a faint smile as he climbed in, but he said nothing more.

'As for the rest of you,' growled the colonel. 'Now you've fixed your bike, you can get off my property. And I'll thank you all not to come back here again.'

They did not wait to be told a second time. Charlie scooped up Sherlock and placed him in the basket and they quickly pushed their bikes out through the gates. The colonel kept watching them until the gates had completely closed. Then the black car pulled away smoothly, tyres crunching up the gravel drive.

'Wow, can you believe *that*?' said Max, as they watched the car disappear towards the house. 'He was even scarier than the housekeeper.'

'I've never seen such unfriendly people,' agreed Charlie. 'And that boy was the most spoiled brat I've ever met.'

'Well, I felt sorry for him,' said Joe. 'He spends all day with that horrible housekeeper and even his dad doesn't seem to like him very much. And now he's going to be sent to a military school that sounds worse than St Grimshanks.'

Lucy checked her watch. 'We should get going,' she said. 'We're supposed to be at the next campsite by lunchtime.' She climbed onto her bike. 'I must say, though, I'm quite glad Byron's not coming with us. I've never come across anyone so rude and boastful.'

Max and Charlie got on their bikes and cycled after Lucy, but Joe lingered for a moment, looking back at the old house. Joe had been struck by just how much he seemed to have in common with Byron. He understood exactly how a person might be boastful if they were desperate to make new friends, because he had been the same before he met Lucy, Max and Charlie.

He would have liked to help Byron, but it didn't look like there was anything he could do. With a heavy sigh, he mounted his bike and began to cycle after the others.

9

CLOSE ENCOUNTERS

The four children made slow progress after leaving Byron's house. For one thing, the path that led to the forest was mostly uphill and, for another, the battery on Max's bike had gone completely flat and he was having to pedal for the first time.

Several times they had to stop and wait for him to catch up and, on one occasion, he lay down by the side of the path and refused to get up until Lucy revived him with tea from her flask and half a bar of chocolate.

'Go on without me,' he whispered in a dramatic voice. 'Leave me behind for the wolves and save yourselves.'

'Stop being so melodramatic,' said Lucy. 'It's only another ten minutes to the campsite but we'd better hurry in case Finnegan gets there before us.'

Eventually, they coaxed Max off the ground, and resumed the ride. After a short while they reached the top of the hill, from where it was a flatter ride to the forest. 'I think this is quite near the place where they spotted a UFO,' said Joe excitedly. 'Who knows, Max, maybe your little green men will come back to try and kidnap you again?'

'The little green men are welcome to kidnap me,' groaned Max. 'Just as long as they don't expect me to pedal the spaceship.'

They reached the campsite as the late afternoon sun was going down. Just as before, Lucy had picked out a perfect clearing in the trees, close to a brook of clear running water.

The campsite was not deserted, however. There was a battered car parked in the clearing with mismatched paint on one of the doors and a coat hanger instead of an aerial. Leaning against the car in his red polyester tracksuit was Mr Finnegan, looking at his watch.

'Oh, no,' said Lucy, under her breath, as they dismounted. 'This is all we need.'

Mr Finnegan tapped his wrist meaningfully. 'And what time do you call this, exactly?' he said in a nasally tone. 'You are nine minutes and forty-three seconds late arriving at a planned checkpoint, Miss Yeung. And that means I am duty-bound to fail the lot of you.' He gave them a nasty smile.

'We're really sorry, sir,' said Lucy. 'We had to stop and fix a puncture. We're only a little bit late – couldn't you let us off?'

Mr Finnegan could scarcely conceal his glee. 'Let you off?' he exclaimed, his voice rising to a squeak. 'I'm afraid I have to obey the rules, Miss Yeung. You are all late, which means that you have all failed.'

'Well, that suits me,' said Max, flinging his rucksack to the ground. 'I've had enough of this outdoor lark anyway.' He strode towards Mr Finnegan's car. 'So where would you like me to sit, sir? The front or the back?'

Mr Finnegan blinked. 'Eh, what are you talking about, Green?'

'It's in the rules, sir,' said Max, opening the passenger door. *'The examiner is responsible for ensuring that any child who fails the exercise is returned to a place of safety.* So, if we've all failed, that means you've got to take us all home, sir.'

Max bent down to peer inside the car. 'If you don't mind, I prefer to sit in the front. But I hope you're not fussy about your seats; I think I might have sat down in a cow pat back there.' He moved to get into the car.

'What? Hang on a minute,' spluttered Mr Finnegan. He shooed Max away from the car. 'I can't have you getting cow poo all over my car.'

Max shrugged helplessly. 'I can't help that, sir,'

112

he said. 'After all, you have to obey the rules, don't you? Oh, by the way, you might want to watch out for Sherlock; he gets very car sick.' Sherlock barked at the mention of his name and wagged his tail vigorously, not looking in the least like a dog that got car sick.

Mr Finnegan looked like he was in shock. He looked at Max and then at Sherlock and then at the others, who were busy trying to stifle their laughter. Then he scowled at Max. 'You think you're very clever, don't you, Green?' he snapped.

'Well, actually, yes,' began Max. 'I am quite—'

'Shut up!' Mr Finnegan was quivering with suppressed rage. He took a deep breath, then straightened up and smoothed out the wrinkles in the polyester. 'Alright then,' he said eventually. 'I have decided *not* to fail you on this occasion, but I'm warning you: put one more foot out of line and I'll call your parents and get them to come and pick you up.' He checked his watch again. 'I expect to see you arrive on time at the final checkpoint and I will *not* tolerate any more lateness. Now get on and make camp.'

He gave them a final glare and then got into his car and drove off, pulling away so fast that he sprayed mud and gravel behind him. As the car disappeared down the track, the group breathed a sigh of relief.

'That was fantastic, Max,' said Joe. 'How do you remember all that stuff in the rule book?'

Max shrugged. 'It's like I always say,' he said. 'If you want to outwit a teacher, it helps to have a child genius along for the ride.'

Charlie made a face. 'How on earth do you manage to ride a bicycle with a head as big as yours?' she said.

They all laughed. 'Well, I think you were brilliant,' said Lucy. 'I thought old Finnegan was going to fail us all for sure that time.'

'You're welcome,' said Max. 'And seeing as I just saved you all from being sent home, I was wondering if—'

'We're still not carrying your stuff,' said Lucy firmly.

They spent the next hour pitching camp. They were much quicker at putting up their tents this time, all except for Max. His tent had been rolled in a ball and tied to the back of his bike so that it was now covered in mud and ripped in places. The guy ropes were tangled and one of the tent poles had gone missing.

In the end, Max simply tied the remains of the tent up in a tree as a sort of makeshift shelter and then laid out his sleeping mat and the slee-backet on the ground beneath it. When he had finished, he stood back and dusted off his hands. 'Much better,' he said. 'Who wants to be trapped inside a musty old tent when they can sleep out in the fresh air?'

Charlie, Joe and Lucy had finished pitching their own tents and Charlie was now throwing sticks for Sherlock, who was retrieving them from the stream. Joe was pulling ingredients from his rucksack to make a meal while Lucy collected dry sticks for the campfire.

'Hey, I can see Byron's house from here,' she said, pointing through the trees. The large red-brick house was clearly visible in the distance and there was smoke coming from one of the tall chimneys.

'At least someone is keeping warm tonight,' said Max. 'Lucky old Byron.'

'I wouldn't be too envious of Byron if I were you,' she replied. 'I felt really sorry for him living in that huge house with no one his own age for company.'

'And what about that housekeeper?' chimed in Joe. 'If I lived with her, I think I'd run away from home.'

'If you lived with her, she'd probably let you,' said Max with a grin.

'Well, we should just be grateful that we've got each other for company,' said Lucy, returning with an armful of dry wood. 'Ahhh... Sherlock! Do you have to do that?'

Sherlock had climbed out of the stream and was shaking himself dry, showering all of them with his doggy wetness. 'Sorry,' said Charlie. 'I'd try to stop him but, to be honest, I think he does it deliberately.'

'OK, Joe, what are we eating?' said Max, rubbing his hands together as he sat down at the campfire. 'Nothing like a massive trek through the wilderness to get your appetite up.'

Joe had placed a saucepan on the camping stove and had emptied in tinned tomatoes and vegetables. While the pan was heating up, he was cutting a loaf into thick, uneven slices.

'I've got a special treat for you tonight,' he said.

'Joe Carter's campfire hash. I've chopped up some vegetarian sausages to go in it too.'

'Sounds great,' said Max. 'And what about pudding?'

Joe stopped slicing and grinned. 'Ah, for dessert I will be making my *pièce de résistance.*' He lowered his voice to a whisper. '*Fried jam sandwiches!*'

Max's eyes opened wide and his jaw dropped open. 'Fried jam sandwiches?' he repeated. 'Is that really a thing you can do?'

'You'd better believe it,' said Joe. 'This is going to be the best thing you've ever eaten out of doors.'

Joe was right. His special campfire hash was thick and warming and just the thing after a hard day of cycling. They ate everything in the pan and mopped around their plates with the bread until there was scarcely any need to wash them. The fried jam sandwiches were an even bigger hit, hot and sweet and sticky and so filling that no one even had room for a toasted marshmallow afterwards.

'Joe, you're a cooking genius,' gasped Max as he

lay on his back by the fire after they had finished eating. 'Who knew that you could eat so well when you're camping.'

'I agree,' said Lucy. 'This trip has been the best. I'm going to be really sorry when we have to go home.'

'Me too,' said Joe quietly. 'As soon as I get back, I have to start getting ready for St Grimshanks. This is the last adventure we'll ever have together.'

Joe sighed and looked down at his shoes while the others exchanged guilty glances. They had been so busy having a good time that they had forgotten Joe would shortly be leaving for boarding school. The gloom fell across the camp like a damp blanket.

'Well,' said Joe, breaking the silence. 'I guess I'm going to turn in. We've got another big day tomorrow.' He got up and headed for his tent.

'Me too,' said Charlie. 'Sherlock went off to bed ages ago. He's probably taking up the whole sleeping bag by now.'

When Charlie had gone, Lucy cleaned her teeth from her water bottle and prepared to turn in while

Max lay by the fire, looking up at the night sky. 'Lucy?' he said quietly.

'What is it, Max?'

'It won't be the same after Joe goes to boarding school, will it?'

'I don't think it will, no.'

Max bit his lip. 'Do you think it will be the end of the After-School Detective Club?'

Lucy was silent for a while. 'I hope not,' she said. 'But I really don't know. Good night.'

'Night, Luce.'

That night it rained.

Fat pellets of rainwater spattered the campsite and ran in rivulets off the tents while the wind howled through the trees. Max woke to a steady drip of water on his face.

He quickly discovered that his makeshift shelter had collected a large pool of rainwater and that it was now dripping onto his slee-backet. When he sat up, he bumped against the bulging nylon so that cold water cascaded down on top of him.

He cursed out loud and scrambled up off the ground to survey his shelter. The ruins of his tent hung down from the branches like the remains of a long-dead animal, funnelling rainwater onto his sleeping mat like a broken water main.

He waddled over to the trees and stood shivering under the thickest branches. The slee-backet had soaked up so much water that it was now twice its normal weight and it clung damply to his skin. He thought of waking the others to see if he could share one of their tents. But Lucy and Joe only had one-man tents and he seriously doubted whether Sherlock would be keen on sharing with anyone except Charlie.

With a heavy sigh, Max waddled a bit further into the forest, reasoning that the thicker branches might give him more shelter from the rain. But if anything the rain seemed to be coming down even harder in the trees than it was out in the open.

He was about to return to the camp when he

stopped in his tracks. The strange light from the previous night had returned. Just as before, the bright light appeared in the distance, low to the ground and making quick changes of direction.

Max's heart began to beat harder in his chest. Part of him wanted to return to the camp and tell his friends, but then he remembered how Joe had laughed at him for being afraid of 'little green men'. He frowned and began to move towards the light. If he was going to wake everyone up, then he was first going to make sure he knew what he was looking at.

At the edge of the forest, he paused. The light was moving backwards and forwards across the marshes, as though it was looking for something. He could hear a sound now too, a powerful throbbing noise that came and went over the noise of the wind. He tried to get a better view, but his glasses had become fogged with rain.

He tried drying his glasses on a damp corner of the slee-backet but when he put them back on, he had a shock. The strange lights had moved closer. It looked like they were coming straight towards him. He gulped; surely they couldn't see him here in the trees?

The strange noise grew louder: a powerful *whooshing* that throbbed and pulsed over the sound of the rain. A strong wind blew up, bending the tall branches of the trees and stirring the leaves into a whirlwind around his feet. Max shielded his eyes from the wind. The noise had become deafening and the lights were now so bright that he could not look directly at them. There was no doubt in his mind now. This was definitely an alien spaceship!

He was about to flee back to the camp when his blood ran cold. A figure was running towards him, silhouetted against the lights, arms flailing as it ran. Was this *an alien?*

Max stood frozen to the spot. His mouth opened and closed but he could not scream; he tried to run but his legs would not work. He watched helplessly as the figure ran straight towards him and collided headlong with him, sending them both sprawling on the ground.

Max screamed and the strange figure screamed. But then Max stopped screaming. The strange figure was not an alien; it was a boy. What was more, it was a boy he knew.

'Byron!' he shouted over the whooshing noise. 'Byron, is that you?'

Byron Hecklegruber was in a terrible state. His clothes were torn and muddy, his hair was in disarray and one of the lenses on his glasses was broken. His eyes were wild with fear and he looked around in blind panic. When he saw Max, he grabbed hold of the slee-backet with both hands and shook him.

'Help me!' he screamed at Max. 'You have to help me. They're coming for me! They want me to go with them.'

'What's going on, Byron?' shouted Max. 'Who's coming for you?'

Byron turned and looked back the way he had

come. The bright light was almost on top of them now, sweeping towards them as the wind and the noise grew to an overwhelming level. 'Too late!' shrieked Byron. 'They've found me!'

Before Max could stop him, Byron scrambled to his feet and fled through the trees as through he was being pursued by a monster. Max tried to follow but, almost immediately, he tripped over the slee-backet and fell flat on the ground. When he looked up, he caught a glimpse of Byron fleeing through the trees. The bright lights abruptly changed direction and began to follow the boy.

'Byron!' shouted Max over the wind and the rain. 'Come back!'

He clambered to his feet and began to grope his way through the trees after the boy, following Byron's footprints in the muddy ground. The slee-backet sagged around his ankles and he had to keep stopping to wipe the rain from his glasses. After a couple of minutes, he had lost sight of the boy and the strange lights altogether.

Finally, he reached the edge of the trees and found himself looking down a long stretch of sloping grassland to the marshes. The muddy footsteps came to an abrupt halt but there was no sign of Byron anywhere. Then he saw the lights again. They were a long way off in the distance now, staying close to the ground and moving away fast.

Max's legs felt weak and he leaned back against a tree to gasp for breath. There had to be a simple explanation for the bright lights, the violent wind and the strange disappearance of the boy. But however hard he struggled to come up with an answer, he kept coming back to the same inescapable conclusion.

Byron Hecklegruber had been kidnapped by a UFO!

10

THE HUNT FOR BYRON

Max was not sure how he managed to find his way back to the camp. He struggled blindly through the forest, his vision blurred by the rain on his glasses, throwing terrified looks over his shoulder in case the aliens were coming back for him.

He was close to exhaustion when something small and white came scampering out of the darkness, barking wildly. 'Sherlock!' gasped Max. 'Thank goodness it's you.'

He fell to his knees in the mud and hugged the little dog as Sherlock covered him with wet licks.

A moment later three torch beams came through the trees towards him and Charlie, Joe and Lucy arrived, looking concerned.

'Max!' cried Lucy. 'Are you okay? We woke up when we heard all the noise, but you'd disappeared.' She looked at the sodden remains of the slee-backet hanging around Max's shoulders. 'What happened to you? You look like you've been swimming in the swamp.'

'A-a-a-aliens!' blurted Max by way of a reply.

'Aliens again?' said Joe. 'The boy's delirious. That can happen when someone spends too long in the wilderness, you know.'

'Shut up, Joe,' said Lucy. 'We need to get him back to the camp before we do anything else. He's freezing cold.'

When Lucy said this, Max realised that he *was* freezing cold. In fact, he was colder than he had ever been in his life. His teeth began to chatter, and he started shivering uncontrollably.

He allowed himself to be led back to the camp,

where they all sat in Charlie's spacious tent while Lucy found him a towel and a dry change of clothes from his rucksack. It had stopped raining, so Joe was able to light the camping stove and make some hot chocolate while Charlie gathered up Max's wet clothes and dumped them in a heap outside the tent.

As he hugged Sherlock and sipped hot chocolate, the warmth returned to Max's bones. He told them about the strange lights and the noise and the wind. Then he told them about meeting the terrified Byron Hecklegruber and how the boy had disappeared without a trace.

'So it really *was* aliens!' said Joe excitedly. 'I told you so. These forests are famous for them. They've taken Byron back to their planet in a flying saucer.'

'There's no such thing as flying saucers, Joe,' said Charlie scornfully. 'You read too many comics for your own good.'

'Well, how do you explain what I saw?' said Max.

'It certainly looked like a UFO, and Byron has definitely disappeared. What else could it be?'

'I don't know what you saw,' said Lucy. 'But Byron could be in really bad trouble. We should call the police.'

'We're not supposed to use the mobile phone unless it's an emergency,' said Joe.

'Well, I think an alien abduction qualifies,' said Charlie. 'Max, you're the one with the phone. Where did you put it?'

'Don't worry, it's perfectly safe,' said Max. 'It's in the pocket of my slee-backet for safekeeping.' He paused when he saw the horrified looks on the faces of the others. Then he followed their gaze to the slimy heap of sodden clothes piled up outside the tent.

They scrambled outside and dug through them until Max found his phone in a waterlogged pocket of the slee-backet. When he held up the device, a trickle of muddy water drained out of the bottom. He tried to turn it on, but the phone stayed stubbornly dark and as dead as a brick.

'Oh, no!' gasped Joe. 'Our last connection with the outside world, gone! We're doomed!'

'Don't be so dramatic,' said Lucy. 'We'll just have to go and look for help. I'm sure we can find someone with a phone we can use.'

'We could go back to Byron's house,' said Charlie. 'It's only a couple of miles.'

'Good idea,' said Lucy. 'We'll leave our stuff here and just take the bikes. It won't take us long to get there.'

'Okay,' said Max. 'But, please, can we wait until it's daylight? I really don't want to spend any more time running around this forest in the dark.'

'That makes sense,' said Lucy. She checked her watch and was surprised to find how late it was. 'It should be light in an hour,' she said. 'We'll leave as soon as we can see where we're going.'

They spent some time gathering the things they would need for the short trip in their backpacks. The slee-backet looked like something that had been blocking a drain and it could no longer be worn so Max was forced to borrow a sweater from Joe. Then Lucy handed around some of her protein snack bars. 'Take these for later,' she said. 'We don't know when we'll get a chance to eat again. Max! What are you doing?'

'Just keeping up my blood sugar,' said Max as he stuffed the last of his protein bar into his mouth. 'It helps with the shock.'

They huddled in Charlie's tent until the sky had lightened enough to see where they were going, then they set out back along the track towards Byron's house.

No one spoke as they pedalled through the still morning mists. The paths were muddy and rutted after the storm, but it was downhill most of the way. In less than half an hour they found themselves standing at the iron gates of Byron's house. There was no one about, but a thin pencil-line of smoke was rising from one of the chimneys.

'Well, someone's home,' said Joe.

There were two vehicles in the driveway of the house: the black car that Byron's father had been driving and a van with darkened windows that had not been there the night before.

'So, what now?' said Charlie.

'Try the intercom?' said Joe. There was a small metal grille and a bell by the gate. Joe leaned on the bell for several seconds.

Nobody answered but, after a long silence, the metal gates swung open silently. 'I guess that's an invitation to go in,' said Lucy.

They started up the driveway, wheeling their bikes over the gravel. There was still no sign of anyone in the house but as they drew closer, the front door opened and Mrs Bukowski stepped outside to meet them.

Mrs Bukowski was no longer dressed as a housekeeper. She wore a black rollneck sweater with dark trousers and black lace-up boots. The children hesitated; she looked lean and fit, and very much like someone who was not to be tangled with. She stood in the driveway with her arms folded.

'What do you want?' she snapped.

The four children stopped on the drive and Sherlock gave a low growl. Charlie bent down to place a restraining hand on his collar. 'We're sorry to bother you so early,' said Lucy politely. 'But we're very worried about Byron.' She looked at the others. 'Max saw Byron in the forest last night. He seemed very scared and then...' Lucy paused, not quite knowing how to say the next part. 'He... sort of... disappeared. Could we come inside and call the police?'

At the mention of the word 'police', Mrs Bukowski

narrowed her eyes and gave Lucy such a poisonous glare that the girl stepped back in shock. The hackles rose on Sherlock's neck and Charlie instinctively tightened her grip.

'You are mistaken,' said the woman coldly. 'Master Byron was here all night. This morning he and his father left early to go on holiday. They will not be back for several days. Thank you for your concern. Now please go.'

Max frowned. 'But I saw him,' he piped up. 'He was terrified. He said they were coming to get him. He said—'

'Quiet!' snapped the woman. 'I have no time for your childish tales. The colonel has gone away with his son and he asks that you do not attempt to visit them again. Now please leave!'

The children exchanged confused glances, then Lucy jerked her head to indicate that they should go. Reluctantly they began to wheel their bikes back down the driveway. Charlie turned and looked back to see Mrs Bukowski still watching them with her arms folded. *Making sure we leave*, thought Charlie. She took a last look up at the house and then paused and peered more closely at one of the upstairs windows.

'Come on, Charlie,' called Joe. 'You don't want to get stuck in this place when the gates shut.'

Charlie sprinted the last few yards up the drive and darted out just as the gates started to close. 'Well,' said Lucy, 'what a horrible woman. She wasn't in the least bit interested in what we were saying.'

'And I don't believe a word of that story,' added Joe. 'How could Byron have been here all night when Max saw him in the forest? And why would he and his father decide to go away so suddenly? It just doesn't sound true to me.'

'It isn't true,' said Charlie suddenly. 'Listen, when we were leaving, I looked back at the house and I caught sight of a face at that upstairs window in the front. The thing is, I think it was Byron.'

'Are you sure?' said Lucy.

'I only saw him for a moment but I'm about as sure as I can be,' said Charlie. 'And he looked strange. Like he was really *scared*.'

'So, what do we do now?' said Max. 'We still don't have any way of calling the police.'

'And what would we say to them even if we did?' said Joe. 'We can't exactly say we thought Byron had been kidnapped by aliens but it turns out he's locked in his bedroom. They'd laugh at us.'

They stood outside the gates for several minutes, pondering what they should do next. Mrs Bukowski had gone back inside the house and there was no sign of Byron's face at the window. From the outside it looked as though the house was deserted.

'Well, I'm not satisfied,' said Lucy eventually. 'There's something fishy going on here.'

'I agree,' said Charlie. 'That woman's definitely up to no good. Sherlock hated her on sight.'

'Maybe we should watch the house,' said Joe. 'You know, like they do in the detective movies.

That way if there is something strange going on, we might have something to report to the police.'

'Actually,' said Max, 'that's not a bad idea.' He pointed to a copse of trees on a low hill, a short distance from the house. 'Perhaps we could hide up there in the trees and keep watch with Charlie's bird-spotting binoculars.'

'What about Mr Finnegan?' said Joe. 'If he checks up on us again then he'll fail us all for sure.'

'It can't be helped,' said Lucy. 'Whatever is going on here is more important than the Duke of Wellington awards. Our friend Byron needs help and the After-School Detective Club are coming to his rescue.'

11

THE UFO

They agreed that the best thing to avoid suspicion was to cycle away from the house as though they were leaving. They followed the curving path along the riverbank until the house disappeared from view behind a rise in the land. Then they cut across the fields and doubled back towards the forest, wheeling their bikes across the muddy terrain.

It was nearly an hour before they arrived at the copse of trees that looked down on the house. They left their bikes far back in the trees and then crawled on their bellies through the bushes until they had a clear view of the house.

Sherlock was a little puzzled by what they were doing but if this was a game, he was determined to join in. He crouched low and crept through the undergrowth on his own belly, looking up at Charlie as they went.

'This is great,' whispered Joe, as they lay on their stomachs, looking at the house. 'It feels just like being a secret agent.'

'What it feels like,' complained Max, 'is being muddy and wet through. I'd only just got warm and now my trousers are soaked again.'

'You have to expect a little discomfort when you're doing detective stuff,' said Joe. 'I mean, where would we be if we just gave up every time it got a bit damp?'

'I can't speak for you, but I'd be at home in bed,' grumbled Max.

'Shut up, the pair of you,' hissed Lucy. 'Charlie, can you see anything?'

Charlie squinted through her binoculars. 'Not really,' she said. 'The car and the van are still in the driveway, but I can't see anyone about. Wait a minute...'

'What is it?' they all said at once.

'It's that woman, Mrs Bukowski. And there's a man with her.'

'Is it Byron's dad?' said Lucy.

'I don't think so,' said Charlie. 'They're getting something out of the van.' She put down the binoculars. 'Now they've gone back in the house. I couldn't see what they were taking inside but it definitely looked suspicious.'

'How do we know they're not just having the place decorated?' said Max.

'That man didn't look like a decorator,' said Charlie. 'He was dressed in black and he looked like a bodybuilder.'

'It's all pretty odd,' said Lucy. 'But we should stay here until we have something more definite to tell the police.'

They agreed to take turns keeping watch through the binoculars. Charlie volunteered to go first while the others crept back and made a temporary camp in the trees. Lucy gave Sherlock some of the dried food from his back pouch while Max took off his trousers and hung them up in a tree to dry.

Then Joe unwrapped one of Lucy's protein bars and shared it out between them, including a piece for Sherlock, who, despite having just eaten, wolfed it down without even seeming to chew it. An hour later, Charlie returned with nothing to report. 'The house is completely quiet,' she said.

'You'd never know there was anyone in there.'

Lucy took a turn keeping watch, followed by Joe. As it drew closer to lunchtime, Max reluctantly took the binoculars and crawled through the undergrowth to take his turn. His stomach growled as he crawled, reminding him of how hungry he was. He wondered just how long they were going to keep watching a house where nothing seemed to happen.

No sooner had he taken up position at the edge of the trees than he jumped up again with a loud yell. He had lain down on a large stag beetle, which had promptly nipped him through his clothes. Seconds later, Lucy, Charlie and Joe burst through the bushes.

'What's going on?' cried Lucy. 'Did you see something?'

'It's nothing,' said Max grumpily. 'Just a close encounter with the local wildlife, that's all. Honestly, how much longer do we have to do this—'

He was cut off mid-sentence by Joe, who was

gesturing frantically. 'Max, you're supposed to be keeping watch. There's someone down there, look!'

Three figures had emerged from the house and were standing in the driveway. The children immediately threw themselves to the ground as Max twiddled with the focus on the binoculars. 'There's three of them,' he said eventually. 'Mrs Bukowski and the big guy that Charlie saw. The other one is Colonel Hecklegruber.'

'So much for the story about him going on holiday,' said Joe.

'What are they doing, Max?' said Lucy.

Max adjusted the focus. They were too far away to hear anything, but it looked to Max like there was an intense conversation going on. Mrs Bukowski seemed to be very annoyed. She was frowning and exchanging angry words with the colonel, jabbing him in the chest with her finger as she talked.

'It doesn't look good,' said Max. 'Mrs Bukowski seems to be furious with the colonel. If I didn't know better, I'd say she was threatening him.

He looks pretty angry too.'

'Angry' was something of an understatement for the way the colonel looked. Even through the binoculars, Max could see that the man's face was pale and his lips were clamped into a thin line.

Abruptly, the colonel climbed into his car and pulled away from the house. The gates swung open and the car swept out of the drive, disappearing quickly down the track. Mrs Bukowski and her accomplice waited for the gates to close before returning to the house.

'What did you see?' said Joe eagerly, when Max put down the binoculars.

'The colonel looked furious,' he said. 'But there was something else too. He looked frightened, as if something bad was going to happen.'

'That's just how Byron looked when I saw him at the window,' said Charlie.

'And now he's left his son alone in the house with those people,' said Lucy. 'Something's really not right here.'

'Can we go to the police now?' said Max wearily. 'If I have to lie in the mud any longer, I'll start growing webbed feet.'

'We still don't have very much to give to them,' said Joe. 'Even if we could persuade them to go to the house, that woman would probably just give them the same story she gave us.'

'Joe's right,' said Charlie. 'Maybe we should get a bit closer and see if we can see anything through the windows? It might give us a better idea of what's going on before we call the police.'

After a brief discussion they agreed they would go down the hill and approach the house from the side where they could not be seen. They collected their bikes and wheeled them back through the forest, following a line of low bushes that kept them hidden from the house.

When they reached the corner of the walled garden, they paused. The walls were a lot higher than they had appeared from a distance and even

Joe and Lucy weren't tall enough to climb them. 'This is no good,' said Joe. 'We can't see the house at all from out here.'

'Let's follow the wall down to the river,' said Charlie. 'It's a bit lower down there. We might be able to see over the top.'

They left their bikes beside the track and followed the wall down towards the river. About halfway down, a small thicket of trees grew close to the boundary. One of the longer boughs extended out over the wall.

'Quick, help me up,' said Joe. 'We should get a good view from up there.'

Charlie and Max gave Joe a foot up into the lower branches and did the same for Lucy. Then Joe and Lucy reached down and helped the others up into the tree. Sherlock stood at the bottom, peering up at Charlie and whining softly.

'It's alright, you daft dog,' she called down to him. 'I'm not going anywhere. Just stay there and keep on guard in case anyone comes.'

At the words 'on guard', Sherlock pricked up his ears and began to patrol the bottom of the tree with his nose close to the ground, searching for strange scents. Sherlock had no idea what he was supposed to be on guard for, but whatever it was, he was going to be ready for it when it came.

The children climbed higher in the tree and a short while later they were all perched on different branches, peering over the wall. Max sat with his arms and legs wrapped tightly around his branch and his eyes screwed shut. 'Really, I'm not that good with heights,' he said in a tight voice. 'Could I go back down and keep watch with Sherlock?'

'Stop complaining,' hissed Charlie as she raised her binoculars. 'There's still no sign of any activity in the house.'

'Hey, look over there,' said Joe, pointing. 'I'm pretty sure that wasn't there yesterday.'

A short distance away, inside the wall, a piece of machinery had been partially covered with a tarpaulin. The machine looked large and spindly but it was impossible to tell what it was under the covers. 'We should get a better look at that,' said Joe. 'I'm going down to see what's under the tarpaulin.'

Before anyone could stop him, Joe shifted his body from the branch to the top of the wall. Then he swung his legs over and dropped to the other side with a soft thump. 'Joe, you idiot,' hissed Max. 'How are you going to get back up again?'

Joe did not answer. He crept towards the covered machine and lifted a corner of the tarpaulin to look underneath. 'Hey, Max,' he called out. 'I think I've found your UFO. Look at this.'

He pulled at the heavy sheet, which slid away to reveal a delicate-looking craft with a narrow tail and long rotor blades. It looked like a large black insect that had landed on the grass.

'A helicopter?' gasped Max.

'This must have been what you saw last night,' said Joe. 'Look, there's even two large floodlights underneath it.'

'That explains the lights in the sky and the wind in the trees,' said Max. 'Whoever was flying this must have been chasing Byron.'

'Who would chase someone in a helicopter?' said Lucy.

Joe seemed very excited to have discovered the helicopter and was now peering through the smoky glass windows. 'I know loads about planes and helicopters,' he said. 'I've seen one like this at the airfield where my dad takes his flying lessons.' He shielded his eyes with both hands and stuck his face closer to the glass to get a better look. 'That's the radar and over there is the transponder and that big stick they use to steer it is called the "cyclic".' He looked up and them and grinned. 'I reckon I could fly this myself with a bit of practice.'

Max snorted. 'No one is going to let you practise with their helicopter anytime soon, Joe. But at least now we know what was chasing Byron.'

'I agree,' said Lucy. 'I think we've seen enough to tell the police what we know, now.' She looked up at the sun, which was sinking steadily towards the west. 'We should get going before it starts to get dark.'

'Uh-oh,' said Charlie, peering through the binoculars. 'We've got trouble.'

The front door of the house had opened and Mrs Bukowski stepped out with the big man. Charlie watched them intently and then gave a little cry of alarm when the woman raised her own binoculars to look straight back at them. Mrs Bukowski turned and said something to the man, who immediately began to sprint across the lawn towards them.

'She's seen us,' cried Charlie. 'Let's get out of here.'

'Joe!' cried Lucy. 'Get back up here, quick!'

Joe looked at the man running across the lawn towards him and darted back to the wall, but it was too high for him to reach, and he couldn't get a foothold to clamber up. He glanced over his shoulder and saw the man had covered half the distance already.

'Joe, grab hold of my hand!' cried Lucy.

Joe did not need telling twice; he jumped up and caught Lucy's hand. The girl grunted and gritted her teeth as he scrambled up the wall and managed to get one arm over the top. Then he swung his legs up and they both jumped down on the other side, seconds before the man arrived.

'Come on, quick,' yelled Charlie. 'Everyone back to the bikes. Let's go, Sherlock.'

The four children and the little dog raced to the spot where they had left their bikes. Charlie dumped Sherlock in the basket and they quickly pedalled away from the house, as fast as they could.

'That was too close for comfort,' gasped Joe.

'We're not out of the woods yet,' said Lucy. 'We need to make some distance in case they decide to come looking for us.'

'Too late!' cried Max. 'Look!'

They turned to see the iron gates swinging open and the black van skidding wildly as it turned out onto the rough path. The van accelerated along the track towards them, spraying mud and gravel as it came.

'Pedal faster!' cried Max.

They stood up on their pedals to pick up extra speed, but it was no use. Moments later, the black van passed them before turning sharply across their path and sliding to a halt.

The four bikes came to a stop as the van doors were flung open. Mrs Bukowski and the big man jumped out and came towards them, looking angry and grim-faced. 'I'm really sorry,' blurted Joe as they approached. 'We didn't mean any harm. I'm just interested in helicopters, that's all.'

'Joe's right,' said Lucy at once. 'We promise we won't come back if—'

'Silence!' The woman's voice was as cold and sharp as broken glass and they fell quiet immediately. 'You are all in very serious trouble.' She turned to the man. 'Ivan, put them in the van. And take their bikes too. I want no trace left behind.'

The man called Ivan opened the doors and began to shove them roughly towards it. But when he grabbed Charlie by the arm, Sherlock started barking madly and bared his teeth. Ivan aimed a kick at Sherlock, who scampered out of the way, still barking furiously. Fearful for her dog, Charlie leaped on Ivan, her eyes blazing.

'Leave my dog alone!' she yelled. She punched Ivan in the chest as hard as she could manage but the blow seemed to have no effect. Ivan's response was simply to scoop up Charlie and shove her into the back of the van.

Sherlock immediately redoubled his barking,

snapping furiously at Ivan's heels and making a tremendous din. When he had put Charlie down, Ivan picked up a heavy tyre iron from the back of the van and took a step towards the little dog.

'Stop it, you fool!' Mrs Bukowski's voice was so sharp that Ivan stopped what he was doing and turned to look at her. 'Stop antagonising the dog before someone comes to find out what all the noise is about. Just leave it behind and get the kids in the van. Now!'

Ivan scowled at Sherlock and then turned to the rest of the children with a furious glare. 'All of you, get inside,' he growled. 'Do it now! I won't tell you again.'

They needed no further persuasion. Lucy, Max and Joe clambered into the van and sat down on the hard metal floor next to Charlie. Then Ivan lifted their bikes and tossed them in. He slammed the back doors shut with a bang and then threw a last poisonous glance at Sherlock,

who continued barking but wisely stayed out of the man's reach.

Mrs Bukowski and Ivan got back inside and the van performed a rapid U-turn before driving back towards the house. As soon as they started moving, Charlie clambered across the bikes and pressed herself against the back window.

She cried out when she saw Sherlock standing alone in the middle of the track and kept watching the little dog until the van turned in to the driveway of the big house. As the big gates shut behind them, Charlie put her head in her hands and sobbed.

While the black van crunched its way up the gravel drive, the other three children exchanged terrified glances. Max gulped. 'Well, I guess that settles one thing,' he said.

'What's that?' said Lucy.

'I think we've definitely failed the Duke of Wellington awards.'

12

KIDNAPPED

The setting sun made the river glow like a molten ribbon as the black van crunched to a halt outside the house. Ivan yanked open the rear doors of the van and pulled out the bikes, piling them on the grass while Mrs Bukowski pointed at the children.

'Get out! All of you.'

They clambered out quickly, shivering in the chill air. Charlie had stopped crying and her face had become cold and serious. She glared at Mrs Bukowski, though the woman did not seem to notice.

'You've got no right to do this,' said Charlie angrily. 'I demand you give us back our bikes and open those gates.'

Mrs Bukowski scowled. 'I have every right to do this,' she snapped. 'You and your friends were caught trespassing on this property and we saw you interfering with a valuable helicopter.'

'We weren't interfering with it,' piped up Joe. 'I only wanted to have a look at it. We didn't do it any harm.'

'We'll let the police decide that,' said Mrs Bukowski. 'You're all going to come inside with us while we call them.'

'Well, that's fine with us,' said Lucy, stepping forward bravely. 'We'd be very happy to meet the police and tell them what we know.'

'Enough talking,' said Mrs Bukowski. 'Come with me.' She led them towards the house, then jerked her head towards the open door. 'Everybody inside, now!'

The inside of the house was dark with wood panelling and tiled floors. There was a wooden staircase and a gallery running around the first floor. The air smelled heavy with wood polish.

The four children gathered in a sullen group in the hallway as Mrs Bukowski shut the front door. 'Liliana!' she shouted. 'Lili, where are you?'

'What is it?' called back an angry voice. A powerful woman with cropped black hair and a stern expression emerged from a wood-panelled sitting room at the end of the hall. She had broad shoulders and muscular forearms and wore a green flight suit with the sleeves rolled up. Even though she was indoors, her eyes were hidden behind a pair of sunglasses with mirrored lenses.

'What's all the shouting for? I was having a nap.' She spoke in the same clipped tones as Mrs Bukowski. She stopped when she saw the children and looked them up and down. 'What's this, Commander?' she said. '*More* kids? Are you collecting them or something?'

'Shut up, Lili,' snapped Mrs Bukowski. 'Take them upstairs to the bedroom and put them with the other one. I don't need them getting in my way right now.'

Liliana folded her arms and frowned at Mrs Bukowski. 'Why *me*?' she demanded. 'I'm a trained pilot, not a babysitter. Why not get Ivan to do it?'

Mrs Bukowski's expression twisted into one of complete fury. 'Because I'm telling *you* to do it!' she snarled, baring her teeth.

For a moment, she looked so utterly terrifying that Liliana backed away with her hands raised in surrender. 'Alright, alright,' she said at once. 'I'll do it, I'll do it. No need to get so excited.' She looked at the children and gave a weary sigh. 'Okay, you heard the commander. Get upstairs. Now!'

They began to climb the stairs with Lili following close behind. She led them up to the gallery and stopped in front of one of the bedroom doors. She fumbled with a bunch of keys, then opened the door and jerked her head. 'Get inside,' she muttered.

The four friends looked at the open door and hesitated. 'We want to see the police as soon as they get here,' insisted Lucy. 'We've got a few things to tell them about you too.'

Lili turned to look at Lucy so that the girl could see her own image reflected in the mirrored lenses. 'The police?' chuckled Lili. 'Oh yes, the police. Well, don't worry. As soon as they get here, I'll make sure to come and tell you straight away. Now hurry up and get in there. Believe me, you do not want to upset the commander any more today.'

The door shut behind them and the key turned in the lock. The four friends looked at each other nervously. 'Why has she locked us in?' said Joe.

'I'm not sure,' said Lucy. 'But I don't like it one bit.'

'I hate to say this,' said Max in a small voice. 'But I'm not convinced that the police are coming anytime soon.'

They looked around and saw they were standing in a brightly lit bedroom overlooking the front lawns of the house. There was a computer on the desk and the floor was littered with clothes, computer games and books. At the sound of their voices, there was a movement in the corner of the room and Byron's head popped up from behind the bed. He adjusted his glasses and peered in their direction.

'Who's there?' he said.

'Byron!' said Joe, excited to see a familiar face. 'It's us. We came to rescue you.'

Lucy and Max exchanged glances. They could hardly describe what they were doing as a rescue, given that they had now been locked in the bedroom along with Byron.

The boy got up from the floor, rubbing his eyes and staring at the children as though he thought they might disappear. 'It *is* you,' he said eventually. 'I thought I was dreaming.'

'You're definitely not dreaming,' said Lucy. 'It really is us. How long have you been locked in here?'

Byron sighed. 'Since last night,' he said. 'I've been going out of my head with boredom.' He looked them up and down and frowned. 'But what happened to you? It looks like you've been swimming in the marsh.'

They looked down at their sodden clothes and realised it was true. A full day spent lying on the ground in the woods had left them filthy and mud-stained. Joe shrugged. 'It's a long story,' he said. 'But tell us what's going on. Who are those people downstairs and where's your dad gone?'

Byron ran his hands through his fair hair. 'That's a long story too,' he said. 'Why don't we sit down?' He perched on the end of the bed while Lucy and Joe sat on the floor and Max settled into a squashy beanbag. Charlie took herself to a corner of the room and stared out of the window, taking no part in the conversation.

Byron told his story in a hushed voice, with several glances at the door, as though he was afraid that someone might be listening outside. He seemed much less confident and boastful than he had done when they had last met him.

'The other two arrived in the helicopter, yesterday evening, after you left,' he said. 'They landed in the grounds and Mrs Bukowski let them in. Dad demanded to know what was going on but Mrs Bukowski threatened him. She said that if he didn't do exactly what they said, they'd make him sorry.'

'So, what did they say?' said Joe eagerly.

Byron bit his lip. 'I didn't understand a lot of it,' he said. 'But they told Dad they were going to keep me here as a hostage and that if he didn't do what they wanted, he'd never see me again. Dad said he thought they had guns. He was really worried.'

Lucy turned pale. 'That's terrible,' she said. 'But what do they want, Byron? Why are they doing all this?'

Byron shook his head. 'It's all to do with my dad's work,' he said. 'Somehow, they found out that Dad is one of the pilots who's been testing the new jet fighter. They want him to steal some of the top-secret plans kept at the air force base.'

'Top-secret plans?' said Joe breathlessly. 'You mean they're spies? Actual spies, like in the movies?'

Byron shrugged. 'I guess so,' he said. 'Dad was always really worried about security; that was why he'd never let me have any friends over. But I always thought he was making a fuss about nothing. I never thought real spies would turn up at our house.'

'That would explain why they keep calling Mrs Bukowski "Commander",' said Lucy. 'They must be working for a foreign government.'

Byron was starting to look really worried now. 'Spies? Foreign governments?' he said in a wavering voice. 'You don't think they're really going to take me away, do you? I might never see Dad again.' They saw that the boy's eyes had filled with tears.

Lucy smiled kindly. 'I expect they just said that to scare you,' she said. 'They'll go as soon as they get what they want. I don't think they really mean to kidnap you.' She was trying to sound reassuring, but in truth the people downstairs seemed ruthless enough to do anything.

'Go on with the story,' said Joe. 'What happened after that?'

Byron wiped his eyes and continued. 'First they cut the phone lines,' he said. 'Then, they tied us up and kept us downstairs for hours until it was time for Dad to go to work.'

'But I saw you,' said Max. 'Last night in the forest. I thought you were being chased by a UFO.'

Byron winced at the memory. 'Yeah, you did,' he said. 'I persuaded them to untie me so I could go to the bathroom. Then I climbed out of the window and made a run for it. I remembered you guys said you were camping in the forest and I didn't know where else to go. But then they got in their helicopter and came after me.'

'So it *was* the helicopter I saw?' said Max.

'Yeah. They've got some sort of special camera on it that lets them see in the dark. They found me really easily and brought me back here. They were really angry after that. They locked me in my room and they threatened to hurt my dad if I tried to escape again.'

He began to cry and buried his face in his hands. 'I didn't know they'd get that angry,' he said. 'I couldn't bear it if they hurt Dad. I know I complain about him but since Mom died...' He paused and swallowed. 'They didn't hurt him, did they?'

'We saw him leaving while we were watching the house earlier,' said Lucy. 'It looked like he was going to work.'

Byron's eyes widened. 'You were watching our house?' he said.

'Sure,' said Joe. He pointed out of Byron's window. 'See those trees up there? We were camped out all morning with Charlie's binoculars.'

Byron looked out of the window and his jaw dropped open. 'So that's how you figured out what was going on?'

They nodded.

Byron wiped his eyes and, for the first time, he smiled. 'Wow, you guys are totally awesome,' he said. 'So, when are the police getting here?'

The friends exchanged glances and Max looked down at his feet awkwardly. 'We *wanted* to call them,' he said slowly. 'But I was the only one that had a phone and it got waterlogged in the rain. So, we came here to see if we could use the phone.'

'Then Mrs Bukowski said she was going to call them,' added Joe. 'But they locked us in here instead.'

Byron's expression changed as he listened. His face dropped and his mouth fell open. 'Wait a minute,' he said. 'Are you telling me that *no one else knows you're here?*'

They nodded glumly. Byron threw up his hands in exasperation. 'Oh, well, that's just *great!*' he cried. 'Some useless rescuers you turned out to be. How dumb *are* you people?'

Charlie exploded out of her seat in the corner.

'You've got no right to get angry with us,' she yelled. She strode across the room and jabbed at the startled Byron with her forefinger. 'We came here because we were worried about you and we wanted to help. But all you can do is complain like a spoiled brat. I wish we'd never bothered; we should have just left you here and finished our expedition. At least we'd all still be together.' She went back to the window and stood with her arms folded, staring out with a furious scowl.

Byron looked at her with a bewildered expression and then turned to the others. 'What did I say?' he said. 'What's wrong with her?'

Lucy frowned at him. 'Well, you were pretty rude to us,' she said. 'And Charlie's worried about Sherlock. Those people left him wandering around on his own out there.'

'Oh, I see.' Byron bit his lip and was quiet for a moment. 'Well, I guess I was a bit rude,' he began.

'A *bit*?' said Lucy, raising an eyebrow.

'Alright, I was very rude,' he said. 'I'm really sorry.

I guess I'm just not very good at having friends.'

'Maybe you should practise a bit more,' said Joe. 'Friends aren't so difficult once you get the hang of it. Perhaps you should start by apologising to Charlie?'

Byron thought about this for a bit and then he walked over to where Charlie was standing. 'I-I'm sorry,' he said hesitantly. 'About what I said earlier.' Charlie did not look at him. 'It's just that... no one ever tried to rescue me before,' he continued. 'And I'm sorry that Sherlock got left behind. But I'm sure he'll be OK, I mean, he's a pretty smart dog.'

Charlie turned a fraction to look at Byron and the hard line of her mouth softened a tiny bit. 'He *is* a smart dog,' she said.

Byron nodded eagerly. 'He really is,' he said.

'And you really are a spoiled brat,' said Charlie. Byron stared dumbfounded at the girl and then he caught the faintest of smiles at the corner of her mouth.

He gave a nervous laugh. 'Yeah, I guess I am sometimes,' he said. 'But I promise when we get out of here, I'll help you look for Sherlock. He can't have gone far. So, do you forgive me?' He held out his hand. Charlie looked at it suspiciously and then she shook it briefly.

'Well, thank goodness that's settled,' said Joe. 'So, what do we do now?'

'Well, I can't just sit around doing nothing,' said Lucy. 'We should try and find a way to escape.'

'I'm not so sure, Luce,' said Max. 'if the choice is between tackling Mrs Bukowski or staying here...' He settled back in the bean bag. 'I'll go with safety and comfort every time.'

'But we can't just let them get away with it,' said Joe. 'Lucy's right. We have to try and break out of here and tell the police what we know. Is there anything we could use as a weapon?'

'I've got an electric marshmallow toaster,' offered Max, patting his rucksack. 'But I think it's going to take more than that to tackle a gang of ruthless international spies.'

Lucy looked out of Byron's bedroom window.

Darkness had descended and only the lights of the house illuminated the gravel drive. She looked down uncertainly and wondered if she could climb down. Lucy was very good at escaping from her own bedroom window, but it was a good ten-metre drop to the ground and there were no drainpipes or trellises that she could get an easy foothold on. 'I don't think we can get out that way,' she said.

Joe looked over her shoulder. 'What about if we tore up Byron's bedsheets and tied them together to make a rope? I saw them do that in a movie once.'

'They wouldn't be strong enough for us to climb down,' said Byron. 'And besides, I don't have enough sheets on the bed to reach all the way to the ground.'

'How about tunnelling our way out?' said Joe.

'We're on the first floor, Joe,' said Max. 'Traditionally, people start digging tunnels at ground level.'

'Well, there must be *something* we can do,' said Joe, exasperated. He slumped down on the bed and put his head in his hands.

After a few moments, Max spoke up. 'Byron, when we were here yesterday, didn't you say there was a hidden chamber in your bedroom?'

Byron nodded. 'Sure, there is,' he said. 'It's behind my wardrobe, but I don't think it will be much help.' He opened the built-in cupboard in the corner of the room to reveal a space stuffed with hangers, shirts, jeans and piles of grubby sneakers.

He pushed aside the clothes and banged around inside for several seconds. Then he tugged hard at something and they heard a soft scraping noise as the back of the wardrobe slid sideways to reveal a dark space.

'There you go,' he said, standing back to let them see. 'The estate agent said the house is over five hundred years old and the people who built it were involved in all sorts of plots and rebellions against the queen. They made this to hide people

175

in case the soldiers came looking for 'em.' He grinned. 'Pretty cool, huh?'

'Yeah, pretty cool,' agreed Joe, bending down to look inside. The space was dark and spidery and lined with rough bricks. 'So, where does it go?'

'It doesn't go anywhere,' said Byron. 'It's just a hiding place.'

Joe looked disappointed. 'Well, what use is that?' he said. 'We need a secret passage that leads outside. That thing's no use to anyone.'

'I'm not so sure,' said Max. He picked up a pair of jeans that Byron had discarded on the floor and pulled on them to test their strength. 'You've got a lot of clothes here, Byron,' he said. 'And they might be just the thing to get us out of here.'

Joe scratched his head. 'I don't see how Byron's old trousers are going to help us.'

Max grinned and tapped the side of his nose. 'Trust me,' he said. 'I've got a plan.'

13

ESCAPE!

The sound of breaking glass was sudden and loud in the quiet of the big house. Downstairs in the sitting room, Liliana's heavy boots clunked down from the coffee table as she sat up straight. 'What was that noise?' she said, startled.

Ivan's massive bulk shifted on the sofa where he had been sleeping. 'Eh, what?' He sat up and rubbed his eyes. 'Sounded like it came from upstairs. You should go and take a look.'

'*I* should go and take a look?' Lili frowned at her companion. 'I'll have you know I'm a skilled pilot. You're just the hired muscle. *You* go and take a look.'

Ivan gave a contemptuous snort. 'What is the matter, Lili? Are you afraid the little children might overpower you?'

Liliana bared her teeth at the big man. 'Look here, you great ox—'

'Why are you both sitting in here doing nothing?' Mrs Bukowski stormed into the room, wearing a look of thunder, and the pair immediately jumped to their feet. 'I don't pay you to argue about who is more important. Get upstairs and find out what that noise was. NOW!'

Lili and Ivan both bolted for the door, becoming momentarily stuck in the doorway in their hurry to get through. They charged up the stairs, followed by Mrs Bukowski, who waited patiently while Lili fumbled with the key.

They pushed their way into Byron's bedroom, then stopped and stared. The double windows were smashed and broken. Shards of glass and splintered wood littered the floor and the curtains stirred in the night breeze.

Byron's wardrobe had been emptied and, all around the room, bedclothes, shirts and trousers lay shredded and torn. Mrs Bukowski went to the window and looked out.

A rope of knotted material, made of sheets, jeans and shirts had been tied to the window frame and dangled all the way down to the ground. She scanned the darkness around the house but there was no sign of the children anywhere.

She whirled to face her two accomplices. 'You fools!' she spat. 'All the time you were arguing, they were getting away. If that boy escapes, we have nothing to bargain with. Now get outside and find them.'

Ivan threw up his hands. 'Find them how?' he said.

'Look for them!' screamed Mrs Bukowski. 'Turn on the floodlights, take torches, search the grounds. If you can't find them, take the van and drive around. They can't have gone far.'

Lili and Ivan scrambled downstairs, falling over themselves to get out of the front door. Mrs Bukowski surveyed the wreckage of the room and swore under her breath. Then she turned on her heel and strode out of the room.

The room fell silent as the sounds of the search moved outside. Then came a faint scuffling from the back of the wardrobe followed by the scrape of a hidden panel being pulled aside. A moment later, Byron tumbled out of the cupboard, followed by Lucy, Joe and Charlie.

'Watch where you're putting your foot, idiot!' hissed Charlie.

'I can't help it,' whispered Joe. 'I've got cramp in my leg. Max was practically sitting on top of me the whole time we were in there.'

Lucy stretched out the crick in her neck and groaned. 'That chamber is barely big enough for one adult,' she said. 'I doubt it's ever had that many people inside it before.'

'It certainly fooled those spies, though,' said

Byron with a grin. He looked like he was enjoying himself immensely. 'That was a great idea of Max's. Max? Where are you?'

There was a frantic scrambling from inside the wardrobe and Max fell out, twisting and writhing and trying to reach the back of his collar. 'Somebody, help me,' he gasped. 'Spider!'

Lucy helped Max to shake a tiny spider from the back of his shirt. He shuddered as he watched the little creature scuttle away and then collapsed onto the beanbag. 'I thought I'd suffocate in there,' he gasped. 'Especially after Joe farted.'

'I did not fart!' squeaked Joe indignantly. 'It's just a bit... musty in there, that's all.'

'Stop bickering, you two,' said Charlie from the window. 'Look, they're leaving.'

They rushed to the window to see the black van pulling away from the house with its headlights on. It paused at the gates and then turned out of the drive, spraying gravel across the lawn as it went.

'They're heading towards the village,' said Lucy. 'We should grab our bikes and go in the other direction as fast as possible.'

They made their way out onto the first-floor gallery and Byron pressed a finger to his lips as they listened. After the drama of the last few minutes, the old house was now eerily quiet. Only the clunky ticking of an old grandfather clock disturbed the peace. 'I think the place is deserted,' whispered Byron.

They proceeded down the stairs on tiptoe until they reached the tiled hallway. 'Our bikes are still out on the front lawn,' said Lucy. 'Byron, go and get yours and then meet us by the front gate.'

'Sure thing,' said Byron. 'I'll see you there.' Then he grinned. 'I haven't had this much fun since we moved to England!' They all smiled at Byron as he opened the front door. Then they froze.

Standing right outside, wearing her twisted, viper-smile, was Mrs Bukowski. Byron gasped and took a step back.

'So,' she said, following him into the hallway. 'You all thought you'd outwitted me, did you?' The smile widened. 'I guessed you were hiding somewhere, waiting for us to leave, but I am not as easily fooled as Lili and Ivan. And now, I will make you pay.'

Byron backed away as Mrs Bukowski advanced slowly across the hallway. 'W-what are you going to d-do?' he stammered.

The woman seemed to be enjoying Byron's terror. 'Perhaps,' she said slowly, 'after your father returns with those plans, we should take you with us as a hostage. Then we might convince him to steal even more secrets for us.'

Byron's eyes grew wide. 'That's not fair,' he said. 'You said that if we did what you asked, you'd let us go. You promised!'

'I promised?' Mrs Bukowski chuckled. 'What can I say? I am a thief and a liar. Too bad you believed me.'

She lunged at the boy, grabbing him by the collar and shaking him so hard that his teeth chattered in his head. 'Not so keen to escape now, are you?' she snarled. 'Let's see how much you like spending the rest of the day in that cupboard of yours.'

The other four children were shocked into silence. Mrs Bukowski was scary and dangerous, and seemed capable of almost anything. But the sight of Byron being so terrorised made Lucy's blood boil. 'Leave him alone, you bully!' she cried.

Before Mrs Bukowski knew what was happening, Lucy had grabbed her wrist, and was trying to prise it off Byron's collar.

'Everybody, help Lucy!' yelled Joe. He grabbed hold of Mrs Bukowski's other arm and held on tight. Meanwhile, Charlie jumped onto the woman's back, wrapping her legs around her and pulling on her ears.

Mrs Bukowski screamed and fought back furiously under the assault. She jerked her arm free from Joe's grip, sending the boy stumbling across the hallway. Joe collided with the hall table, knocking over a large vase, which exploded on the hard tile floor and sent shards of porcelain skittering in all directions.

Mrs Bukowski proved to be surprisingly strong. Still keeping a tight hold of Byron's collar, she reached up and pulled Charlie off her shoulders with her free hand, sending the girl sprawling on the floor. Then she grabbed Lucy's wrist and twisted it painfully.

'You little monsters,' she snarled. 'I will teach you all a lesson you won't forget. I'll... *aaarrrgh!*'

Mrs Bukowski shrieked suddenly and leaped high into the air. As she landed, one of her boots came down on a piece of broken porcelain and her feet slid out from underneath her. She landed heavily on her back and struck her head on the hard floor with a dull crack.

Mrs Bukowski groaned, moved once, and then lay still. The others turned to look at Max, who was standing across the hallway wearing a look of wide-eyed terror. In his hands he was clutching a long fork with widely spaced prongs.

'Electric marshmallow toaster,' he explained with a weak smile. 'Apparently it's just the thing for tackling ruthless international spies. Who knew?'

The others stared and then Joe began to laugh. 'Max, I don't believe you finally found a use for that thing,' he cried. 'You really are a genius.'

Max was staring at the woman, lying motionless on the hall floor. 'She's not... *dead*, is she?' he said in a hushed voice.

Lucy crouched down to get a closer look at Mrs Bukowski. 'No. It looks like she's just knocked herself out,' she said. 'But we should get away from here before she wakes up. She was mad enough before Max stabbed her in the backside.'

They staggered out into the night air with Joe and Lucy helping Max, who was shaking all over and still clutching the toasting fork with both hands. Outside, there was another surprise waiting for them.

Something small and brown and white scampered out of the darkness towards them, barking wildly as he came. Charlie let out a shriek of delight and fell to her knees. 'Sherlock!' she cried, hugging the little dog tightly. 'He must have wriggled through the gates. Good boy, *good* boy!'

Sherlock yipped and barked and covered Charlie in wet slobbery licks to make absolutely sure that she understood just how happy he was to see her. And when he was quite certain that she had got the message, he ran to each of the children in turn to make sure they got it too.

Byron went to collect his own bike and returned, wheeling it around the side of the house. 'Okay, let's go,' he said. 'Before Mrs Bukowski wakes up again.'

No one needed to be told twice. They picked up their bikes from the spot where Ivan had dumped them, and Charlie placed Sherlock in the front basket. Then, turning on their lights, they made their way down the gravel drive. They stopped at the gates and waited expectantly for Byron to open them.

The boy patted his pockets and then began to search through each of them in turn. Then a horrified expression crept across his face. 'Oh no,' he said. 'The electric gate opener! I left it in my bedroom.'

Everyone groaned. 'Byron, you idiot!' snapped Charlie. 'How are we supposed to get out? Now someone will have to go back and get it.'

They all looked back at the house. 'I don't think anyone should do that,' said Lucy. 'What if that woman has woken up? There must be another way out of here?'

Byron shrugged. 'I don't think so. The house is surrounded by the wall on three sides and by the river on the other side. There's no way to get out.'

'Don't you have a boat or something?' said Max. 'Perhaps we could escape that way?'

Byron shook his head. 'I wanted to get a boat when we moved here but Dad wouldn't let me.' Then he brightened. 'Wait a minute,' he said. 'We don't have a boat, but what about the old swimming platform? It's just a raft made of planks and oil drums but we might be able to use it to get to the other side of the river.'

'Well, let's get a move on,' said Max anxiously. 'I don't want to be here when Mrs Bukowski wakes up and remembers who stabbed her with a marshmallow fork.'

They remounted their bikes and pedalled furiously down the sloping lawns towards the river. They gave the house a wide berth but there was no sign of any movement inside. At the bottom of the slope, they got off their bikes and squelched through the mud towards the river, taking their bicycle lights to use as torches.

Lucy shone her light over the water, and they saw the rickety swimming platform they had seen from a distance the day before. The raft floated about ten metres from the bank and was constructed of soggy brown wood, lashed to some half-submerged oil drums. A faded red flag drooped limply from a pole in one corner.

'You want to cross the river on *that*?' said Max. 'It doesn't look like it would carry Sherlock, let alone the rest of us.'

'More importantly,' said Charlie, 'how do we get to it?'

'We could swim,' offered Joe. 'It's not very far out.'

Byron looked embarrassed. 'I can't swim,' he said. 'I never learned. I have to wear water wings when we come out here in the summer.'

'How can you not know how to swim?' said Charlie scornfully.

'Alright,' said Lucy, giving Charlie a warning look. '*I'll* swim out and get the raft. Max, hold my stuff.'

Lucy took off her rucksack and handed it to Max and then stripped down to her shorts and T-shirt before wading out into the river. 'There's about six inches of mud on the bottom,' she said, making a face.

She gasped as the water reached her middle. 'Oh, wow, this is so cold.' She took a few seconds to catch her breath, then leaned forwards and began to swim with a smooth and steady breaststroke.

No sooner had she started to swim away from the bank than the current began carrying her downstream. She adjusted her course and renewed her efforts. It was hard work, and her muscles tired quickly in the cold water but she made steady progress towards the platform.

Finally, she reached out and grasped the thick rope around one of the oil drums, and gave a silent 'thank you' to her dad for insisting that she'd taken swimming lessons when she was little.

The others erupted in a loud cheer as Lucy pulled herself effortlessly onto the wooden platform, then turned to give them a grin. Almost immediately her face fell. 'Oh no!' she cried, pointing back towards the house. 'The gate's opening.'

They turned in time to see a pair of headlights swinging back through the gate and the black van coming up the driveway. 'It's Ivan and Liliana,' cried Max. 'They're back.'

The van pulled to a halt outside the house and the two spies got out. Sherlock recognised Ivan immediately and began barking furiously so that Charlie had to catch him by the collar to stop him charging up the hill. By now the two were looking and pointing in their direction. 'They've seen us,' cried Charlie. 'Hurry up, Lucy, they're coming.'

Lucy fumbled with the line that secured the raft, but the rope was old and waterlogged, and her frozen fingers struggled to unpick the dense knot. She looked up from her task to see two people

sprinting down the grassy slope towards them, torch beams swinging in the darkness. In frustration she bent down and pulled at the wet rope with her teeth until, finally, the knot gave way.

As soon as the platform floated free, the current began to carry it downstream. Lucy hunted around for something she could use as a paddle. She found a loose board on one side of the platform. When she levered her fingers beneath it,

it came up easily with the sound of tearing fibres.

Using the old plank as a makeshift oar, she kneeled on the edge of the platform and paddled frantically. At first the raft circled lazily, reluctant to return to the shore. But then, slowly, it began to move towards the riverbank.

'Lucy, come on!' yelled Joe. 'They're nearly here.' He waded out and grabbed the rope, then started hauling the raft back towards the shore.

By now Ivan and Lili were only yards away and would surely have caught them if it hadn't been for Sherlock. As they drew nearer, the little dog pulled free of Charlie's grip.

The pair were startled by the ferocity of the little dog as he came at them with bared teeth. A look of terror crossed Liliana's face and she ducked behind Ivan. 'Keep that beast away from me!' she yelled. 'I hate dogs!'

Ivan lunged towards the little dog, trying to grab his collar, but Sherlock ran nimbly between Ivan's legs. The big man tried to turn around but only succeeded in tripping over his own feet and falling down heavily in the mud.

Sherlock began barking furiously at Liliana, who was plainly terrified. 'Don't let that animal near me!' she yelled. She tried to run but also slipped on the marshy ground and fell face first into the mire.

By now, Lucy and Joe had brought the raft into the shallows. Joe helped Max and Byron onto the platform, which wobbled dangerously under the added weight. 'Charlie!' yelled Joe. 'Get on!'

Charlie stuck two fingers in her mouth and let out a piercing whistle. 'Sherlock! Here, boy,' she cried.

Sherlock had been running in wide circles around the two spies, barking and snapping, but at the sound of the whistle he turned to his mistress and bounded across the grass. Charlie scooped him up with both arms and waded out to the raft. 'Good boy, Sherlock,' said Joe with a grin as he helped them both to climb on board.

He was about to climb onto the raft himself when something heavy collided with him from behind. For one horrible moment, he plunged beneath the muddy brown waters. Then he surfaced, coughing and spluttering as he was dragged backwards through the water by a pair of muscular arms.

'Got you,' said Ivan.

Joe tried to cry out, but Ivan was holding him too tightly. He struggled to reach the raft, but it had already moved out of his reach. The last thing he saw was the desperate expressions on the faces of his friends, watching helplessly as they floated away.

Joe had been captured.

14

ADRIFT

The others watched, powerless to help, as Joe was dragged from the water by Ivan and Liliana. 'What are we going to do?' gasped Charlie as they drifted away from the bank. 'We can't just leave Joe behind. We have to go back.'

'We can't go back,' said Lucy. 'They'll just catch us too. At least this way we have a chance of getting away and calling the police.' Lucy knew that what she was saying was the sensible thing, but in her heart she wanted to head back to the shore just as much as Charlie did. A horrible, scared silence fell across the group. None of them wanted to think about what might happen to Joe if they didn't find help soon.

The raft drifted into the middle of the river and picked up speed in the current. Very soon the old house had fallen far behind and they were swallowed up by the night. There were no lights on either bank and the silence was broken only by the gentle splashings of the raft and the soft hooting of marsh birds.

For a long time, no one said anything. Then Lucy broke the silence. 'It's really cold out here,' she said, adopting her most sensible voice, 'and we've all been in the water. We should focus on trying to stay warm. It could be a long time before we can get help.'

'I don't mind the cold so much,' said Max. 'But we haven't eaten for hours. Did anyone bring any food?'

'Let's see what supplies we have,' said Lucy. Holding up her bike light, she rummaged through her small rucksack with her free hand. 'I've got some more protein bars,' she said, handing out one each to Charlie, Max and Byron. 'And I've got some tea in my flask and there's an orange and a banana we can eat later.'

Max had some raisins and a packet of crunchy hoops, which had mostly been crushed to powder in the bottom of his bag, and Charlie had a packet of wine gums and some chocolate biscuits. Sherlock was still wearing his doggy backpack containing his dried food and Charlie emptied a small packet onto the wooden boards for him.

Byron shrugged apologetically. 'I'm sorry,' he said. 'I didn't bring any food with me.'

'That's okay,' said Lucy. 'You can share ours.'

'Really?' Byron seemed surprised. 'But you've hardly got anything. Why would you do that?'

'Because it's what friends do,' said Max. 'They share what they have with each other.'

'Oh.' Byron thought about this for a minute. 'I never really had proper friends before,' he said.

'My dad's job meant we had to keep moving around between different military bases. Whenever we got somewhere new, I tried to make new friends, but the other kids never seemed to like me very much.'

'I'm not surprised,' said Charlie. 'You'd have more luck making friends if you weren't so boastful all the time.'

'What do you mean?' Byron flared at her. 'I'm not boastful. You're just jealous of me because your dog likes me.'

'What?' Charlie looked ready to fly at Byron but Lucy intervened quickly.

'I think what Charlie means,' she said quickly, 'is maybe you shouldn't try so hard to make friends all the time. Maybe if you just tried being yourself, people would like you better.'

Byron did not reply. Instead, he scowled at all three of the children then removed himself to the furthest corner of the raft and sat with folded arms, staring out across the river. Lucy sighed;

clearly this was going to be a very long night. She only hoped that Joe was alright.

Joe was quite a long way from being alright.

After Ivan and Lili had pulled him out of the water, they dragged him back to the house. The front door was wide open and the hallway was still littered with broken shards of porcelain, but there was no sign of Mrs Bukowski.

Ivan led Joe into the living room and made him sit on the sofa, then held up a finger to warn him not to make a noise. Joe sat quietly, his heart pounding as he wondered what was going to happen next and whether he would ever see his friends again.

The door to the kitchen swung open and Mrs Bukowski came in. She looked pale and drawn and there was a bandage wrapped tightly around her head. Ivan and Lili stiffened slightly.

'We got him, Commander,' said Ivan, with some pride. 'The others got away. But we grabbed the American kid before he could get on the raft.'

Joe frowned when he heard this. They seemed to think he was Byron, but that made no sense at all. Apart from their blonde hair, they did not look much alike. Then he caught sight of himself in the ornate mirror hanging over the fireplace and saw at once how they had made the mistake. The figure that looked back at him was bedraggled and covered in so much dark mud that Joe barely recognised himself.

Mrs Bukowski gave him such a cold glare that Joe's stomach flopped over. 'So, your friends have gone for help, huh?' she snarled. 'Well, it doesn't matter. As soon as your father gets back with those plans, we will all be gone from here. And you are going to come with us as insurance, in case anyone tries to follow us,' she added.

She smiled, enjoying the look of terror on his face. Then her smile faded suddenly. She crossed the room quickly and squinted more closely at him, cupping his chin in her hand so she could get a better look.

'You fools!' she exploded suddenly. 'This is not the American boy!'

Ivan and Lili had been looking quite pleased with themselves but now confusion filled their faces. 'That cannot be,' said Ivan. 'I pulled him from the river myself. It's him. The blonde boy.'

Mrs Bukowski held up Joe's face so they could both see him more clearly. 'Look at him, you idiots,' she spat. 'He may be blonde but he is not the same kid. You let the American get away.'

The looks of confusion turned to horror as Ivan and Lili realised the seriousness of their mistake. 'It was Ivan's fault,' said Lili at once. 'He was the one that grabbed the kid. I had nothing to do with it.'

'How am I to blame?' protested Ivan. 'One blonde kid looks just like another. How am I meant to keep track of which one is which?'

'Silence!' Mrs Bukowski's voice was like a small explosion. Ivan and Lili immediately fell quiet.

'You two are as useless as a pair of warthogs. If that boy gets away, it will jeopardise our entire mission.'

She grabbed Joe by the hair, so tightly that it hurt. 'Where are they going?' she demanded. 'Tell me now or I'll make it very bad for you.'

Joe swallowed. 'N-nowhere,' he stammered. 'At least, I don't know where they're going. We were just trying to get away.'

'They were on the old raft,' said Lili quickly. 'They're probably drifting downriver.'

Much to Joe's relief, Mrs Bukowski let go of his hair and assumed a thoughtful expression. 'Alright,' she said, after a few moments. 'It's fifteen miles to the next village and they won't have got far on that old raft. Lili, go outside and start the helicopter.' She looked down at Joe and gave him her snake smile. 'We'll take this one with us. If he gives us any trouble, we'll throw him out of the helicopter.'

Mrs Bukowski ordered Lili and Ivan to take Joe

outside and put him in the helicopter while she collected the torches they would need for the search. Poor Joe found himself dragged to his feet again and marched outside to the spot where the helicopter was parked. Ivan pulled off the tarpaulin, while Lili opened the back door and shoved Joe into one of the seats, with firm orders not to touch anything.

While they waited for Mrs Bukowski, Ivan folded the tarpaulin while Lili walked around the outside, making her pre-flight checks. Joe sat in the back seat of the helicopter and shivered, though not from the cold. Surely Mrs Bukowski hadn't meant her threat to throw him out of the helicopter? But when he remembered the woman's cold eyes, he was not sure of anything any more. He gulped and tried to think about something else.

He looked around the cabin and his eyes settled on the door handle. He could open the door and try to make a run for it. But Ivan and Lili would be sure to chase after him and, even if he could outrun them, where would he go? The house was surrounded by high walls except for the part that faced the river, and he couldn't imagine himself plunging into the cold, muddy water in the darkness.

He tried to make himself think clearly. If the spies caught up with the others, there would be nothing to stop them from stealing the secret plans and maybe even kidnapping Byron as well. But if he could stop them taking off, then he might buy his friends some more time.

He looked around again and this time his eyes settled on the complex array of dials and gauges spread across the dashboard. For a moment he toyed with the idea of cutting some wires or damaging the helicopter in some way so that it couldn't fly properly. But a moment's thought made him realise that damaging a helicopter that was about to take off with you inside it was a *really* bad idea.

Then his gaze fell on a box mounted on the bottom of the dashboard. It was something he recognised from watching his father's flying lessons. And, if he remembered correctly, it could be the answer to all of his problems.

He glanced out of the window and saw that Lili and Ivan were still outside, chatting while they waited for Mrs Bukowski. They didn't seem to be watching him too closely. Joe felt his heart beat a little faster. If he was going to act, it would have to be now. Taking a last look outside, he leaned forward in his seat and began to fiddle with the dials on the dashboard.

The river was black. The sky was black. The banks on either side of them were black. After an hour of drifting through nothing but blackness, it seemed to Max as though they were floating on a never-ending sea of night. He lay on his back on the raft, trying not to think about how cold he was or how uncomfortable his wet clothes were and, above all, trying not to think about how hungry he was.

'Do we have any wine gums left?' he asked.

'You ate the last of them an hour ago,' said Charlie's voice in the blackness. 'I've got some of Sherlock's dried food left, but you might have to fight him for it.'

'I've still got an orange if you want to share it?' said Lucy.

Max groaned. 'Fruit, Lucy? You know I don't do fruit. What I really need right now is some hot treacle pudding.'

'With custard,' added Charlie.

'And some of Joe's lumpy hot chocolate,' added Lucy wistfully.

Byron had been sitting in a sulk on a corner of the raft, shivering and looking miserable. But now that the talk had turned to the topic of food, he found himself unable to keep quiet any longer.

'I'm bored, and I'm cold and I want to go home,' he complained. 'How much further is it going to be?'

'I don't know,' said Lucy calmly. 'We left our maps behind, but I think it's still quite a long way to the next village. At least it's beginning to get light. We'll be able to see where we're going soon.' She pointed across the marshes where a pale line of lavender stretched across the horizon and the sky was turning grey. Now that they could see the countryside around them, it was obvious that they were still nowhere near civilisation.

'I *hate* being on this raft!' cried Byron. 'I wish you'd never made me come with you. In fact, I wish I'd never met any of you at all!'

'In case you'd forgotten,' snapped Charlie, 'if it wasn't for us, you'd still be stuck in that house with those people. And while we were helping you to escape, our friend got caught and we've still no idea what's happened to him. Really, you are the most selfish and ungrateful person I've ever met, Byron Hecklegruber!' She got up and stood over Byron with clenched fists, making the raft wobble alarmingly.

Charlie's outburst was so sudden and so fierce that Byron was stunned into silence and he shrank back into his corner. Max and Lucy looked on anxiously, not daring to say anything in the face of Charlie's anger.

In the end, it was Sherlock who made the peace. The little dog did not like it when his mistress was angry, even though this happened quite a lot. He sidled up to Charlie and gave a little whine as he licked her hand. When she looked down, he wagged his tail and his doggy tongue lolled out. Then, to everyone's amazement, Sherlock crossed the raft to where Byron was sitting and licked his face before sitting down beside him.

Charlie stared at her dog, and her jaw dropped open. 'Sherlock, what do you think you're doing?' she demanded.

'I think he's trying to tell you something,' said Max. 'And I think he's right. What we have to do right now is find a way to rescue Joe. And the only way we're going to do that is if we stop arguing and stick together.'

Charlie looked at Max, then at Sherlock, then at Byron. She opened her mouth to speak but, at that moment, the raft shuddered to a sudden stop and tipped alarmingly to one side. Charlie wobbled and would have fallen into the river if Byron hadn't leaned forward and grabbed her by the elbow.

'Oh no,' said Lucy, 'I think we've run aground.'

While Charlie and Byron had been arguing, the raft had drifted steadily towards the reeds at the edge of the river. Now the oil drums underneath the raft appeared to be stuck fast in the mud. 'Try rocking it from side to side,' said Max. 'That might unstick it.'

They tried shifting their weight from one side to the other, but the movement only seemed to drive the oil drums deeper into the silt. After a few minutes of trying, the raft was stuck as solidly as if it had been buried in concrete.

'This is useless,' said Lucy. 'We'll never get it out of this muck. There's nothing else for it – we're going to have to walk from here.'

15

THE HUNT

Joe sat back in his seat and bit his lip, hoping that nobody would notice what he'd done. As soon as Mrs Bukowski came out of the house, they climbed into the helicopter and Lili put on her sunglasses and got ready for take-off.

Mrs Bukowski sat up front with the pilot while Ivan squeezed his sweaty bulk into the back seat next to Joe. Joe had seen helicopters before, but he had never been a passenger in one. And even though he was terrified of what was going to happen, part of him was still excited by the prospect of going for a ride in a helicopter.

Lili flicked a series of switches and the

dashboard lit up with jewelled lights. There was a cough and a whine from the engine and the long rotor blades began to turn, slowly at first, then faster and faster until the thunderous pulse of the blades filled the cabin. There was a shudder as the fragile craft left the ground and the nose dipped forwards sharply. Then Lili pushed forward on the throttle and the helicopter swept across the lawns and out over the river.

Lili was obviously a skilled pilot and she flew the machine expertly, just a few feet above the surface of the flat water as they headed downriver after the raft. Mrs Bukowski shouted instructions over the noise of the rotor blades. She spoke rapidly in a language that Joe could not understand but he could tell well enough that they were hunting for his friends.

In the centre of the equipment console, a small screen showed a grainy black and white picture of the view from outside the helicopter. Despite the fact that it was still night-time, the picture was clear and bright. Joe guessed that this must be the special camera Byron had told them about, the one that could see in the dark.

Joe bit his lip. With a device like that, it would be easy for them to spot his friends afloat in the middle of the river. He only hoped the others had the sense to find a decent place to hide.

'You know, we really ought to find somewhere to hide,' said Byron. 'That helicopter found me real easy last time.' They were traipsing along a narrow footpath that meandered along beside the river. Lucy was leading while Byron trailed miserably at the back.

When they couldn't free the raft, they had waded ashore, making them colder and wetter and miserable all over again. Then they had begun a slow and uncomfortable journey on foot.

'And where d-do you s-suggest we h-hide, exactly?' gasped Max, his teeth chattering like a pair of castanets. 'You couldn't hide S-Sherlock out here.' He paused to look around at the surrounding countryside and he did not much like what he saw.

If they had been hoping that the raft might bring them to civilisation, they seemed to have arrived at the furthest point from it. To their right lay the flat expanse of the river, wandering lazily over the mud flats. To their left was a wide expanse of boggy marshland, thick with tussocky grass and dense brown reeds.

There were no church spires, villages or even a lone cottage where they might go and ask for help. Apart from the scuttling marsh birds, the landscape seemed to be entirely uninhabited.

'I think we're still a few miles from the next town,' said Lucy, looking around. 'But Byron's right. If they come after us in the helicopter, there's absolutely nowhere to hide out here.'

'What about those trees?' said Charlie pointing across the marshland to a thin copse of trees about half a mile away.

'Too dangerous,' said Byron. 'My dad told me

never to cross the marshes. The mud can suck a person under if they're not careful. We have to stay on the track.'

Max groaned and rubbed his backside. 'I never thought I'd miss my slee-backet,' he said. 'I think I've l-lost all f-feeling in m-my b-bum. If I g-get frostbite they m-might have to amputate.'

'No one is going to amputate your bum, Max,' said Charlie. 'You'll just have to put up with the cold for a bit longer. We have to make some more distance before the helicopter gets here.'

'I think it might be too late for that,' said Byron. He was looking back the way they had come and pointing towards the grey horizon. 'Look, there!'

They saw it immediately. A bright light hanging low in the sky, as brilliant as a young star. The light was weaving back and forth across the marshes as though it was searching for something. 'It's them,' said Lucy. 'And they're looking for us. Everybody, run!'

The sight of the helicopter gave them a

renewed sense of urgency. They started to jog along the muddy path, with Lucy trying to keep them moving at a brisk pace. They had gone no more than a quarter of a mile when Max cried out. 'It's no good,' he gasped. 'I'm finished.'

He leaned over and put his hands on his knees as he tried to get his breath. 'You guys, go on without me,' he panted. 'I'll just lie down in a ditch or something. Perhaps they won't find me.'

'It's too late,' said Lucy. 'I think they've found all of us.'

When they looked back, the helicopter was no longer weaving back and forth; it was coming straight towards them. They could see the dark shape of the machine, like a long-tailed insect, and they could hear the incessant *thwop-thwop-thwop* of the rotor blades as they chopped the air.

'What are we going to do?' wailed Byron. 'We can't let them catch us. I don't want to be kidnapped.'

'Don't worry,' said Lucy. 'We're not going to let

anyone kidnap you if we can help it.' But she had a cold feeling in her stomach when she said this, because she didn't see how they could stop it from happening.

Max had gone very quiet when they saw the helicopter. He watched it coming towards them for a few moments, then he looked out across the marshes with a strange expression as though he was doing difficult sums in his head. 'We should run,' he said, pointing across the marsh. 'Over there, towards those trees.'

'I already told you,' said Byron. 'We shouldn't go across the marshes. The mud is too—'

But Max wasn't listening. He was already sprinting down the shallow bank towards the marsh as fast as his short legs would carry him. 'Follow me,' he yelled back over his shoulder. 'And don't worry. I've got a plan!'

From his seat in the helicopter, Joe could see everything that was happening on the ground.

As soon as Mrs Bukowski spotted the other children, she began shouting excitedly and pointing. Lili made quick adjustments to the controls and the engine noise increased suddenly. She pulled on the control stick and the helicopter made a stomach-lurching turn.

Joe could see his friends quite clearly now. They had left the footpath and were running across a flat expanse of rough grassland, apparently heading for a small group of trees. Mrs Bukowski turned to Joe with a look of triumph in her eyes.

'So much for your escape attempt,' she sneered. 'Let's hope your friends see sense and come quietly. I'd hate to have to make an *example* of anyone.' Her mouth twisted into a smile that suggested she would be only too pleased to make an example of someone. 'Lili,' she snapped. 'Take us down!'

The helicopter swooped low over the heads of the four children and turned to hover in the air for a few seconds before settling gracefully onto the soft ground. Before the rotor blades had whined to a stop, the doors were flung open and Lili and Ivan ducked out.

Ivan immediately slipped on the soggy surface and fell on his face, while Lili sank up to her shins in a boggy pool. Mrs Bukowski followed, stepping carefully out of the helicopter. Then she reached into the back of the aircraft and pulled Joe out by his collar.

'Don't just stand there like apes in a zoo,' she yelled at the others. 'Get after those children.'

Ivan picked himself up and lumbered after Lucy and Max like a charging water buffalo. Lucy could have outrun him easily, but Max fell into a boggy pool and she stopped to help him. Ivan was upon them a moment later. With one hand he grabbed Lucy's collar, and with the other he grabbed Max's arm. The two children struggled and kicked as they tried to get away, but the big man just shrugged off the blows as though he didn't feel them.

While Ivan was busy, Lili sprinted after the others. Byron was already some way ahead and close to the trees, but Charlie was beginning to tire. The mud had soaked through her jeans and every step was becoming heavier and more laborious. She looked around just in time to see Lili bearing down on her and she screamed as the woman crashed into her, sending them both sprawling. For a moment, Charlie was completely submerged in muddy water before Lili pulled her up, coughing and gasping for breath.

Ivan and Lili brought the children back to the spot where Mrs Bukowski was holding Joe. She looked carefully at the three mud-soaked children, trying to work out which was which, then she frowned. 'Where's the other one?' she demanded. 'The American? You've let him escape again, you idiots.'

Ivan and Lili looked at each other. 'I thought you had him,' said Lili in an accusing tone.

Ivan scowled. 'Why would I have him?'

he snapped. 'I had my hands full with these two. I thought *you* had him.'

'It doesn't matter what either of you thought!' Mrs Bukowski yelled. 'You let him get away. *Now find him!*' Her voice rose to such a scream that they both immediately turned and started back across the marsh, looking for Byron.

When Byron had seen the other children being captured, he had immediately dropped to the ground. While Mrs Bukowski was talking, he had crawled on his belly into a thick patch of reeds until he was completely hidden.

From the safety of his hiding place, he watched Lili and Ivan wading around in the marsh looking for him. At one point, Lili passed just a few feet away without seeing him. Byron realised that all he had to do was stay still until they gave up and he would be safe.

It was at that moment that Charlie let out a petrified scream. 'Sherlock?' she cried. 'Where's my dog? I can't see him.'

The other children looked around frantically. In all the excitement of being chased by Ivan and Lili, they had lost track of Sherlock. Now the little dog was nowhere to be seen.

'Oh no,' said Lucy. 'I can see him. He's over there.' She pointed to a spot close to where Lili had caught Charlie. There, in the middle of a pool of thick, glutinous mud, they could just make out the brown and white shape of Sherlock's head, sticking up above the surface.

Charlie screamed again. 'He's trapped in the mud,' she cried. 'He'll be sucked under. Don't worry, Sherlock, I'm coming.' She started towards the struggling shape, but Mrs Bukowski grabbed her roughly and shoved her down on the ground.

'Oh no you don't,' she snarled. 'You kids have put me through enough trouble today. Everybody stay here. Your little dog can drown for all I care.'

Mrs Bukowski stood over Charlie, ready to stop her if she tried to go after Sherlock again, and the girl was forced to watch as her beloved dog struggled in the mire. They could hear him whining now as he sank lower in the mud. 'Please!' sobbed Charlie. 'Please let me help him, I'll do anything you ask.'

The others joined in, pleading and begging to be allowed to help Sherlock. But Mrs Bukowski just smiled her evil smile and stood in their way.

Byron watched the drama unfold from his hiding place in the reeds. Lili and Ivan seemed to have given up searching for him now and had stopped to watch Sherlock. Ivan was pointing and laughing.

The blood rushed in Byron's ears as he watched the desperate scene. If he stayed hidden, he would only have to wait until the spies took off in the helicopter before he could make his escape. He would be free!

But, on the other hand, if he stayed hidden, then Sherlock would surely drown and there would be nothing that Charlie or her friends could do about it. Byron didn't want to see Sherlock get hurt, he liked the little dog, but what could he do? He looked from the children to Sherlock and back again. And then, suddenly, with startling clarity, he knew exactly what he had to do.

Ivan let out a sudden shout. 'There's the boy!' he cried. 'Get after him.'

Byron had broken cover from the thick reeds and was scrambling across the uneven ground towards the spot where Sherlock was struggling. His lungs burned as he leaped between the boggiest patches, trying to find firm ground. He glanced over his shoulder and saw Ivan and Lili lumbering after him. He had to get to Sherlock before they caught him, he thought. He just had to.

At one stage he lost his footing and slipped into a thick pool of ooze that sucked at his arms and legs. With the last of his strength, he pulled himself free of the mud and slithered out of Ivan's grasp as the big man tried to catch his ankle.

A moment later, Byron reached the pool where Sherlock was struggling just as the little dog's head sank beneath the surface. The boy plunged straight into the boggy mess and thrust his arms deep into the mud. For a moment he groped blindly in the mire, until his fingers closed around one of the thick straps of Sherlock's doggy backpack. With the last of his strength, Byron heaved.

Sherlock's thickly coated body came free of the mud with a great sucking noise and both boy and dog collapsed, panting, onto the grass. A moment later, Sherlock jumped up and shook himself briskly, spraying mud everywhere. Then, with a happy bark, he bounded on top of his saviour and began to lick the boy's face gratefully as Byron laughed with joy.

A hundred metres away, as they witnessed Sherlock's rescue, the other four children screamed with delight and began to jump up and down and hug each other. 'Charlie, he did it!' cried Lucy. 'Byron saved Sherlock. He's safe.'

Poor Charlie was so overcome that she could barely speak. But she smiled and hugged Lucy as the tears of joy rolled down her face, carving clean channels through the grime.

Mrs Bukowski looked like someone whose fun had just been spoiled. She scowled at the children then shouted to the others. 'Grab that boy. Bring him here.'

Ivan and Lili waded out to the spot where Byron was still being lavishly licked by Sherlock. They pulled him to his feet, still holding Sherlock in his arms, and then led him back to where Mrs Bukowski was holding the other children.

As they drew near, Byron put Sherlock down on the ground and he ran excitedly into the arms of Charlie, who began sobbing afresh as she hugged her beloved pet. 'Thank you, thank, you, thank you,' she kept saying over and over. 'Thank you for saving him.'

Byron smiled bashfully as Max punched him affectionately on the shoulder and Lucy gave him a warm smile. But there was no time for further celebrations. Mrs Bukowski grabbed Byron

roughly by the shoulder and shoved him into
line with the others.

'Your little adventure is over now,' she hissed.
'As soon as the colonel returns with the secret
plans, we will leave and take his precious son

with us as a hostage. As for the rest of you' – she looked at the other children – 'don't think I have forgotten who did this to me.' She pointed to the bandage around her head and glared at Max. 'I will have to think up something special for you.'

Poor Max was so terrified that his knees literally began to shake with fear. Mrs Bukowski smiled to see the fright in his eyes. 'Get these kids in the helicopter,' she barked at Ivan and Lili. 'Then let's get back to the house.' Then she paused mid-sentence and cocked her head to one side. 'Do you hear that noise?' she said with a frown. 'It sounds like... *sirens*.'

16

MAX'S TRAP

They listened.

At first the only sound they could hear was the distant honking of marsh birds and the gurgling of the streams. But then, they heard it. Very faintly at first, then growing steadily louder: a wailing noise that rose and fell on the breeze. The sound was unmistakeable.

'They *are* sirens,' said Max. 'And they're coming this way.'

The three spies began to look around wildly. 'Over there!' said Ivan suddenly. He pointed across the marsh to a line of fast-moving vehicles that had appeared in the distance.

The vehicles were large and bulky, with fat wheels for driving through the mud and were painted in military colours. Their headlights blazed and their sirens wailed like banshees in the distance.

A look of pure horror crossed Mrs Bukowski's face. 'How can this be!' she raged. 'We're in the middle of nowhere. How did they know that we were *here*?' She turned to her accomplices. 'Ivan, get the American boy in the helicopter. Lili, get us in the air as quickly as possible. We'll make his father pay for this treachery.'

Ivan and Lili turned to leave and then stopped in their tracks. 'Commander!' gasped Lili. 'The helicopter!'

Lili's face had turned ashen as she pointed to the spot, fifty metres away, where the helicopter had landed. The long skids that supported the weight of the craft had begun to sink into the boggy ground. The helicopter was now leaning to one side and already the tip of one of the long rotor blades was stuck in the soft mud. The rising marsh water had crept up the sides of the machine and the cockpit was now filling with slime.

Joe let out a low whistle. 'I don't think that helicopter is going anywhere,' he said.

Lucy gave a delighted shriek and clapped her hands. 'Max! *Now* I understand why you wanted us to run into the marsh,' she cried. 'You knew they'd land the helicopter and that the weight would make it sink into the soft ground. You set a trap for them.'

Max grinned and gave a modest shrug. 'All in a day's work for a child genius,' he said.

The sound of the sirens grew louder as the line of heavy vehicles turned onto the footpath, their fat wheels spraying mud high in the air as they raced towards them. Each vehicle was decorated with a winged white star and the words *US Air Force* on the side.

'They're military vehicles!' said Joe. 'They must have come from the airbase.'

Unable to take off in the helicopter, Mrs Bukowski and her accomplices looked around in panic for a means of escape. 'They're coming for us,' yelled Ivan. 'Save yourselves!'

Lili and Ivan began to run across the marshes, slipping and stumbling in the boggy ground while Mrs Bukowski shouted angrily after them. 'Come back, traitors,' she screamed. 'We are not defeated yet.'

The trucks skidded to a halt and a dozen men and women wearing battle fatigues and the blue berets of the US Air Force scrambled out onto the path. A fierce-looking man with steel-grey hair and a ferocious voice began to bark orders in an American accent and a group of airmen started to scramble down the bank.

Mrs Bukowski's eyes widened, then she turned and ran after Ivan and Lili. But she did not get far before she lost her footing and fell, face first into a boggy pool. For a moment she disappeared completely beneath the mud until two tough-looking airwomen hauled her out by the arms.

More of the airmen chased after Ivan and Lili and, in less than five minutes, all three of the spies had been rounded up. While Ivan, Lili and Mrs Bukowski were being bundled into the back of the trucks, the fierce man stood at the top of the bank and glared down at the five children. Joe noticed that he wore sergeant's stripes on his arm.

'And who the blazes are you?' he demanded.

The five children exchanged guilty glances. The sergeant seemed so fierce that none of them wanted to be the first to speak. Eventually Byron stepped forward.

'Please, sir,' he said nervously. 'I'm Byron Hecklegruber. My dad is Colonel Hecklegruber. He works at the airbase.'

The sergeant looked at the mud-drenched figure before him and frowned. '*You're* Colonel Hecklegruber's boy?' he said. He removed his beret and scratched his head. 'So, what exactly are you doing all the way out here with those people? And what happened to that helicopter?' He pointed to the stricken machine, which was now submerged up to its windscreen. 'How about someone starts giving me some answers before I have you all thrown in the guardhouse?'

'There's no need to be so angry,' said Lucy crossly. 'Those people kidnapped Byron and his dad. Then they kidnapped us too.'

'But we managed to escape by hiding in a hidden chamber,' said Max.

'And we got away on a raft,' said Charlie.

'They were trying to steal secrets from the air force base,' said Joe. 'They're obviously all spies.'

The sergeant put up his hands with an exasperated expression. 'Just hold on to your cattle a moment,' he barked. 'Kidnappers?

Hidden chambers? Spies? I have no idea what you kids are on about. All I know is that we had a call from our control tower to say that there was an aircraft in trouble, somewhere in this area. I don't suppose any of you know anything about *that*, do you?'

Joe raised his hand bashfully. 'I'm afraid that's my fault,' he said apologetically. 'They left me alone in the helicopter for a few minutes before we took off.' He swallowed nervously and shifted from foot to foot. 'The thing is, I used to go with my dad when he had his flying lessons, so I know a little bit about the controls. There's a thing called a "transponder", which sends out a signal to identify the aircraft.'

The sergeant frowned and folded his arms. 'I know what a transponder is, son,' he said. 'I've been in the air force for twenty years.'

'Er, yes, right,' said Joe nervously. 'The thing is, my dad told me the transponder is used to send a signal when an aircraft is in trouble. He showed me how to do it one time. So, when I was alone in the helicopter, I changed the code on the transponder to 7500.'

'Which is the international code to signify that an aircraft has been hijacked and needs emergency help,' said the sergeant, nodding.

'Really?' Charlie looked at Joe with new-found respect. 'Wow, Joe,' she said. 'I guess you're not as dumb as you look after all.'

Lucy slapped Joe on the back. 'That was brilliant, Joe,' she said. 'If it hadn't been for you, we'd still be at the mercy of those people. I think Max has got a rival for the title of "child genius".'

Joe grinned broadly, his teeth showing white against his muddy face, but Max was not impressed. 'You call that genius?' he fumed. 'That's just fiddling with a few dials; a little kid could have done it. Don't forget who got them to land in a swamp. Now *that's* genius.'

They laughed out loud at Max's outrage and even Sherlock began to bark excitedly. Then the little dog proceeded to shake himself violently, causing uproar amongst the airmen as they were sprayed with clots of mud.

'Alright, that's enough!' roared the sergeant over the sounds of laughter. His voice was as loud as a jet engine and everyone immediately fell quiet. 'I can see I'm not going to get any sense out of you lot,' he barked. 'But I'm going to get to the bottom of all this if it kills me. I'm taking you all back to the airbase to answer some questions.'

The children groaned. 'Do we have to?' said Lucy. 'We're all freezing cold.'

'And hungry,' added Max.

'And wet,' said Charlie.

'And hungry,' said Max again.

'And tired,' said Joe.

'Did I mention hungry?' said Max.

'Alright, alright, we can take care of all that,' said the sergeant gruffly. 'Now just go with that airman over there and—' He paused. A long black car had turned onto the footpath, being driven at speed.

It slid to a halt behind the trucks, the back door flew open and Byron's father jumped out.

Colonel Hecklegruber was wearing a flight suit and he looked dishevelled and distracted. When the sergeant saw him, he sprang to attention as though his back had suddenly turned to steel.

'Ten-*hut*!' he bellowed. The other airmen immediately followed suit, jumping to attention and saluting their colonel smartly. The colonel himself made a brief salute and hurried past the sergeant to where the children were standing. He scrutinised the five mud-caked figures in front of him.

'Have any of you seen my son?' he said anxiously. 'He's about your age, with blonde hair and glasses.'

'How's it going, Dad?' said Byron cheerfully. He grinned at his father, showing off his braces. 'Did you miss me?'

The colonel's eyes widened and he stared

closer at the muddy swamp creature in front of him. 'Byron?' he said. 'Byron, is that really you?'

Byron's grin widened. 'Yeah, it's me, Dad.' He laughed. 'I'm okay. My friends helped me to escape.'

'My boy!' The colonel let out a great gasp of relief and threw his arms around his son, lifting him into the air and not caring how much mud got onto his uniform. 'Byron. Thank goodness you're safe,' he cried. 'I'd never have forgiven myself if something had happened to you.'

He put the boy down and looked at the others. The four children in front of him were all covered from head to foot in thick grey sludge. Even their dog appeared to be made of mud. 'Do I... know you?' he said hesitantly.

As usual, it was Lucy who spoke first. 'I'm Lucy and this is Max, Charlie and Joe. And that's Sherlock,' she said, her teeth white against the mud. 'We met you yesterday when we were leaving your house.'

The colonel looked slightly dazed. 'That was

you?' he said, looking at them more closely. 'Is it true what Byron said? That you helped him to escape from those people?'

'They sure did, Dad,' piped up Byron. 'They're real heroes, all of them.'

'Not just us,' said Charlie. 'Byron was incredibly brave too. He could have got away, but he came back to save my dog. If it hadn't been for him, poor Sherlock would have drowned.' She swallowed and the tears welled up in her eyes again. 'I don't know what I'd have done if that had happened. Thank you, Byron, you'll always be my hero. Mine and Sherlock's.'

Charlie suddenly embraced a surprised Byron in a very muddy hug. When she finally released him, the boy managed to look embarrassed, even under several layers of mud.

By now Colonel Hecklegruber was looking thoroughly confused. 'You're telling me that Byron... is a *hero*?'

They nodded vigorously. 'He's the best,' said Lucy.

'He can come camping with us anytime,' added Joe.

'You should be proud of him, Colonel Hecklegruber,' said Max.

'Well!' Colonel Hecklegruber began to laugh suddenly and his hard, chiselled face was transformed. 'Byron, my boy, I really *am* proud of you.'

They all grinned as Byron and his father hugged again. Then the colonel turned and gave them all a warm smile. 'You've done us a great service today,' he said. 'But there's still a lot of questions to be answered. Will you all come back to the airbase and help us get to the bottom of what's happened? We can get you all some warm showers and some hot food while you're there.'

'The airbase?' said Joe in an excited voice.

'Warm showers?' said Lucy with a smile.

'Hot food?' said Max with longing in his eyes.

'You bet we'll come,' said Joe.

Only Charlie did not seem enthused by the

idea. 'Aren't you all forgetting something?' she said. She tapped on her watch. 'It's the last day of the expedition. If we're not at the checkpoint by twelve o'clock, old Finnegan is going to fail all of us.'

17

FRIENDS OF THE PRESIDENT

Albert Finnegan checked the list of names on his clipboard and then checked his watch. He leaned back against his battered old car and grinned to himself.

The car park in which he had set up the final checkpoint was busy with parents collecting their children at the end of the four-day expedition. He watched as rucksacks and tents were loaded into boots and tired children climbed into back seats and waved goodbye to their friends.

As the car park gradually emptied, Albert Finnegan felt increasingly pleased with himself.

It had been a brilliantly organised expedition, he thought. No one had got lost or gone missing or broken a leg and every group had arrived at the checkpoint before the final deadline.

Every group except one, that was.

He checked his watch again and smiled grimly when he saw it was now one minute past twelve. Maximillian Green and his irritating little friends had all failed.

He supposed that he would now have to go and find them, which might take hours, and he would probably not have time for lunch in that nice pub he had seen down the road. However, looking on the bright side, he would almost certainly be hailed as a hero for finding a group of lost children. He could see himself now, being congratulated by the headteacher as she gave him a promotion. 'Deputy Headteacher Albert Finnegan' had quite a nice ring to it.

He was still thinking these thoughts when two large military vehicles turned in to the car park.

They were painted in muted, muddy colours and they had fat tyres and metal grilles over the windows. Mr Finnegan saw the words *US Air Force* and swallowed nervously.

The passenger door of one of the trucks opened and out stepped Colonel Hecklegruber, now dressed in his full military uniform, with his cap pulled low over his eyes. As he marched smartly across the car park, he wore a grim, chiselled expression that immediately struck fear into the heart of Albert Finnegan.

'Is your name Finnegan?' the colonel demanded, jabbing Mr Finnegan with an iron-hard finger.

'Y-yes, that's me... sir,' stammered Mr Finnegan. 'What have I done? I mean, whatever it is, I didn't do it.'

'My name is Hecklegruber,' barked the colonel. He jerked his thumb back towards the trucks. 'Got something here that belongs to you,' he said. The back doors flew open and Lucy, Max, Joe, Charlie and Sherlock all clambered out.

Albert Finnegan's mouth dropped open when he saw them. The children were all wearing fresh, grey tracksuits, which carried the logo of the US Air Force and which had been rolled up in the legs and the sleeves. The children all looked clean and well-fed and not at all like a group that had been camping out for three nights. Even their ratty little dog looked like it had just had a bath. And there was another boy with them that he did not recognise, blonde and freckle-faced with braces on his teeth.

'What the devil have you lot been up to?' he demanded as they approached. 'I warned you to stay away from that airbase, didn't I? You wait until the head hears about this.' He turned to the colonel and put on his oiliest and most ingratiating smile. 'I'm so sorry if they've caused you any trouble, Captain, sir. Rest assured they will be properly punished for anything that they've done. Or haven't done,' he added as an afterthought.

The colonel's scowl deepened and Mr Finnegan took a step back. 'It's *Colonel* to you, Finnegan,' said Colonel Hecklegruber. 'And I don't think you understand the situation here, mister.' As he spoke, he kept jabbing Mr Finnegan in the chest with his forefinger so that the teacher feared he would carry a large bruise the next day. 'In the last twenty-four hours, these children have foiled a gang of international spies.'

'S-spies?' repeated Mr Finnegan weakly.

'They prevented the theft of valuable state secrets and they rescued my son from a ruthless gang,' continued the colonel.

'A ruthless gang?' Mr Finnegan reached out to grasp the wing mirror of his car for support and it came off in his hand. He stared at it for a few moments before looking up at the colonel again. 'W-what do you want from me?' he gasped.

The colonel snorted. 'These children tell me that they have to check in to complete their mission. So, here they are. I trust you will pass them with flying colours?'

The colonel ushered the children forward and Mr Finnegan stared, dumbfounded. This had to be some sort of prank, he thought to himself. Except that those uniforms and the trucks looked very real. And that little horror Maximillian Green was looking extremely smug. Mr Finnegan frowned. He should not have to put up with this sort of nonsense from anyone.

'Now, look here, Colonel Huckleblooper,' he began. 'I don't know what story these little toads have been telling you, but they were supposed to be here at twelve o'clock sharp and it is now precisely' – he paused to check his watch – 'three minutes past twelve.' He grinned triumphantly. 'So that means they've failed, Colonel. Sorry, but there's nothing I can do.'

The colonel's face darkened like an approaching thunderstorm. 'No, *you* look here, *Mr* Finnegan,' said the colonel. 'These children have done a great service to your country and to mine. Are you telling me that you *refuse* to pass them?'

Mr Finnegan swallowed hard but he stuck to his guns. 'I d-do,' he stammered weakly.

'Very well then,' said the colonel with a disappointed look. 'If you insist then I shall be forced to make a full report of this matter to my superiors.'

Mr Finnegan frowned. 'Your superiors?'

'I will be filing my regular weekly report to the President this afternoon,' said the colonel. 'And I shall be sure to mention our conversation. Tell me, how many 'n's in Finnegan?'

'The P-President?' gasped Mr Finnegan. 'Of the United States?' He looked as though he might faint.

'The President always insists on hearing bad news straight away,' continued the colonel. 'I wouldn't be surprised if this causes a diplomatic incident.' He turned and began to walk back towards his truck.

'A diplomatic incident?' Mr Finnegan's jaw dropped open. 'Now, hold on a minute.' He scampered along beside the colonel like an agitated puppy. 'Wait, please, Colonel Bucklewrangler. This is all a terrible misunderstanding. I had no idea that *the President* was involved. *Of course* I'll pass them. It's the least I can do for such... *heroes.*'

Mr Finnegan looked like the word almost choked him but he managed to remain smiling. The colonel looked at him with a thoughtful expression. 'You'll pass them all?' he said slowly.

'Yes, yes, of course, Colonel Snootwarbler,' spluttered Mr Finnegan. 'I'm doing it now, look!' He looked down the list on his clipboard and scored four large ticks against the names of the children.

The colonel's frown deepened. 'And what about a special distinction for their bravery?' he said menacingly.

Mr Finnegan stared for a few seconds and then smiled weakly. 'Yes, yes, of course,' he said in a squeaky voice. 'Whatever you like. I'll give them the highest mark anyone has ever had on the Duke of Wellington awards. They'll receive the gold medal for excellence.'

The colonel nodded approvingly. 'Good,' he said. 'Then my work here is done. Thank you, Mr Finnegan. In the circumstances, I will overlook your earlier unpleasantness when I write to the President.'

Mr Finnegan let out a huge sigh and looked like he was ready to collapse in a pool of jelly. The colonel turned to the children and saluted smartly. 'On behalf of the US Air Force, I would like to thank you all for your valuable assistance,' he said sternly. Then, a small smile flickered across his lips and he gave them a broad wink.

As the colonel strode away, Byron dug his hands into his tracksuit bottoms and kicked at the gravel with the toe of his trainers. 'So, I guess this is where I leave you guys,' he said. 'Thanks again for rescuing me. I don't know what would have happened if you hadn't been there.'

'And thanks for rescuing Sherlock,' said Charlie. 'He always liked you. I guess he really is a good judge of character.' At the sound of his name, the little dog barked and Byron bent down to rub him behind the ears the way that he liked.

'It was my pleasure,' he said, laughing. 'And Sherlock really is a smart dog, you know.'

They all laughed. 'You should come and visit us in Southwold,' said Joe. 'You'd always be welcome in the beach hut.'

'Thanks,' said Byron. 'But I don't think I'll be able to. Dad's talking about going back to America to live. He said this whole kidnapping thing made him realise that he'd been too involved in his work and that he and I should spend more time together.' Then he smiled. 'He's really not so fierce when you get to know him better.'

They all hugged Byron, then watched as he ran across the car park to where the colonel was waiting. The colonel put his arm around his son and they both climbed into the passenger seats and waved as the trucks started up.

As the two vehicles pulled out of the car park, Joe leaned over towards Max. 'Do you think the colonel really knows the President?' he whispered.

'I have no idea,' hissed Max. 'But Mr Finnegan believes it and that's all that matters.'

When the trucks had disappeared from view, the children turned to Mr Finnegan. The teacher's face was ashen and he was leaning heavily on his car for support. When he looked up, he realised that all four children were grinning at him.

'So, Mr Finnegan,' said Max, with obvious glee. 'How was *your* weekend?'

18

THE AFTER-SCHOOL DETECTIVE CLUB

Charlie bent her head against the wind and the driving rain as she hurried along the seafront while Sherlock scurried along beside her, looking cold and bedraggled. They passed a line of colourful beach huts, all shuttered and closed, until they reached the last one in the row.

Charlie pushed her way inside and closed the door firmly against the wind. The air inside the little cabin was warm and filled with delicious smells. 'That smells awesome,' said Charlie. 'What's cooking?'

'Joe's making vegetable chilli and toasted

flatbreads,' said Lucy eagerly, from the corner seat. 'I've been watching him do it for the last half an hour and if it's not ready soon I think I'm going to eat my own arm.'

Joe was standing at the small stove, stirring a large pot of something that smelled rich and savoury. 'Be ready in about ten minutes,' he said cheerfully. 'I'm trying out a new recipe to celebrate the end of another adventure.'

Charlie smiled. Joe was never happier than when he was cooking something. 'It sounds amazing,' she said as she took off her raincoat and hung it carefully behind the door. Sherlock had wandered into the centre of the hut and now proceeded to shake himself vigorously, spraying Lucy with cold rainwater.

'Sherlock!' she cried. 'Will you ever learn how to behave properly?'

By way of an answer, the little dog jumped up onto the cushions and curled up in a damp ball beside Lucy. 'Sorry about that,' said Charlie, taking a seat. 'I've been trying to train him but I think he enjoys doing the exact opposite of everything I say. Honestly, he's worse than Max.' She reached into her inside pocket and pulled out an envelope, which she waved in the air excitedly.

'Look what I've got,' she said. 'It arrived in the post this morning. It's a letter from the US Ambassador. He wrote to thank us for helping to stop those spies. He said we were all true heroes.'

Lucy reached into her own pocket and pulled out an identical envelope. 'We all got one,' she said. 'Mum was going to have it framed and put up in the living room, but I told her I'd die of embarrassment. It hasn't stopped her from ringing all my aunts and uncles in Hong Kong and telling them about it, though. It must be costing a fortune in phone bills.'

The door burst open again and Max pushed his way inside. 'It's raining cats and dogs out there,' he gasped. 'No offence, Sherlock. What's cooking, Joe, and more importantly, when can I have some?'

'Vegetable chilli,' said Joe. 'And it will be ready in a few minutes so get out of my way and sit down.'

Max sat next to Charlie and plucked a newspaper from the pile on the table. 'I see we made it into the papers again,' he said, reading the headline. *'After-School Detective Club foil international spy gang.'* He squinted at the picture of them all on the front page, next to a photograph of the helicopter and an aerial shot of Byron's house.

'Look,' said Lucy, 'there's a picture of Byron and his dad, here. They look really happy together.'

'They are,' said Joe as he tasted the chilli and added more salt. 'Byron emailed me last night to say that he and his dad have been getting on really well and his dad's not going to send him to military school any more. He's really pleased about that.'

'I bet he is,' said Max. 'Who wants to spend their time getting up at five in the morning to run around the countryside? Apart from Luce, that is.'

Lucy laughed, then her face fell and her hand went to her mouth. 'Oh, Joe,' she said. 'I'm sorry. I completely forgot that your mum and dad were sending you to boarding school. When do you have to leave?'

Joe gave them a broad grin. 'That's the best part about our adventure,' he said. 'When the story got into the papers, the school wrote to my dad and said it wasn't the sort of publicity a school like St Grimshanks approved of.' He stuck his nose in the air and put on his most pompous voice. *It is with the utmost regret, therefore, that St Grimshanks has no alternative but to withdraw the offer of a place at our school for your son.*

The others all cheered and laughed and banged on the table, and even Sherlock sat up and threw in a few barks for good measure, even though he had no idea what was being celebrated. 'I bet your mum was furious, wasn't she?' said Charlie.

'That's the funny thing,' said Joe. 'She was at first. But then when she saw the letter from the ambassador she seemed really proud. She showed it to everyone at the golf club. Even Dad was pleased because he saved all that money on school fees. So, we were all pretty happy in the end.'

Max was squinting at the newspaper again. 'This article says really nice things about us, even though the photograph makes me look really short.'

'It is an interesting article though,' said Lucy. 'There's a whole piece about Mrs Bukowski. It says here, she heads up a gang of ruthless international spies. They steal top secret military information and then sell it to foreign governments.'

'So, it's true, then,' said Joe. 'They were real spies?'

'Apparently, she's wanted for questioning in five different countries,' said Lucy.

'And we were the ones who caught her,' said Max, leaning back in his seat and folding his hands behind his head.

Joe ferried four steaming bowls of chilli to the table and then placed another on the floor for Sherlock, who began to wolf it down with such enthusiasm that his whiskers were soon thick with gravy. 'Joe, this is the most amazing thing I've ever tasted,' said Max as he shovelled spoonfuls of steaming chilli into his mouth.

'Max, you say that when you eat anything,' said Charlie.

'I know I do,' said Max, through a mouthful of flatbread. 'But I always mean it.'

They ate in silence for several minutes until their bowls were empty and they had mopped up every last morsel of gravy with the bread. Lucy pushed back her bowl with a satisfied smile. 'That was fantastic, Joe,' she said. 'The best end to an adventure ever. I'm so glad you're not going to boarding school.'

'Me too,' said Max. 'Lucy's a terrible cook.'

'Hey!' Lucy jabbed him in the ribs. 'What I was going to say,' she said, 'is that it's brilliant that the After-School Detective Club is going to stay together after all. It looks like the rain is easing up out there. Why don't we celebrate by walking down to the pier and getting some ice creams, my treat!'

'Count me in,' said Max at once. 'I've always said what a great cook you are, Luce,' he added with a grin.

'Thanks. An ice cream right now would be just the thing,' said Joe.

Charlie shook her head. 'I'll have to pass, I'm afraid,' she said. 'I promised to go bird-spotting in the dunes with my mum.'

The others looked at her with startled expressions. 'With your mum?' said Max. 'You never go anywhere with your mum.'

Charlie shrugged. 'I know,' she said. 'But after what happened to Byron and his dad, it got me thinking. I realised that my mum and I hardly do anything together either. If she suddenly wasn't there, then...' She tailed off and was silent for a moment. 'Anyway, I asked her to go bird-spotting with me this afternoon.'

'And she actually said yes?' said Joe.

Charlie smiled. 'She was a bit taken aback when I asked,' she said. 'But I think she was quite pleased. She's even borrowed a pair of binoculars for the occasion.'

'Well, I think it's lovely that you asked her,' said Lucy.

'I thought so too,' said Charlie. 'Right up until the point when she insisted I come to yoga next week.'

They all burst out laughing at the thought of Charlie doing yoga. But they were glad that Charlie was getting on better with her mum. Lucy thought how different she seemed from the angry girl they had first met only six months ago.

As Max stuffed the last piece of bread into his mouth, he suddenly slapped his forehead. 'Wait a minute,' he said. 'I'm an idiot. I almost forgot I had something to show you all.'

He reached into his rucksack and pulled out his laptop, which he placed on the table. 'This isn't going to be another one of your lessons on *Warlocks and Dragons*, is it?' said Joe warily.

Max ignored the comment and opened the computer. 'I was thinking it was about time we started to record our adventures properly,' he said. 'After all, quite a lot of stuff has happened to us this year. We're pretty famous now.'

'Record our adventures how?' said Lucy.

'I've set up our own YouTube channel,' he said proudly. 'I'm going to post a video diary about our adventures so our fans can see them.'

'We have fans?' said Joe, puzzled.

'We might do, one day,' said Max. 'You've got to think big, Joe.'

'So, what adventure have you posted about?' said Charlie, curious.

'This one, of course,' said Max, proudly. 'Watch.'

He tapped some commands into the keyboard and a video bloomed to life on the screen. The scene showed Max sitting behind a large desk with a microphone and a sheaf of typewritten notes in his hand. He was wearing a crisp white shirt with pens in the top pocket and his best bow tie.

'Max, you look like a newsreader,' said Lucy, stifling a giggle.

'Ssh,' hissed Max. 'It's starting.'

Screen-Max shuffled his papers and coughed and then looked directly into the camera with a solemn expression. He really did look like a newsreader. 'Good evening,' he said in a serious voice. 'And welcome to the After-School

Detective Club channel, where we talk about our adventures for all of our dedicated fans out there.'

Lucy groaned and slapped a hand across her eyes. 'I can't believe you actually said that,' she whispered.

Then screen-Max smiled. 'Tonight's adventure is entitled "The Mystery in the Marshes".' He cleared his throat and then he began.

'It all started,' he said, 'with a letter...'

The After-School Detective Club are back in

The Case of the Dastardly Dognappers

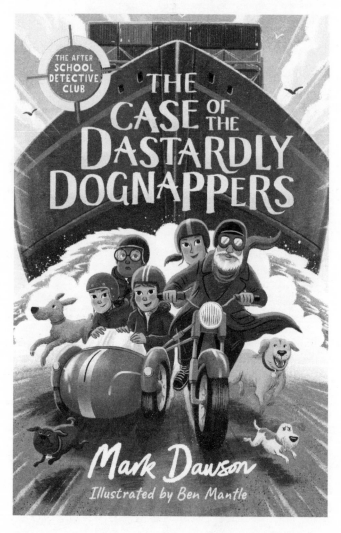

Read on for a preview of the opening chapter . . .

1

THE DINNER PARTY

Joe was arguing with his mother, and it was not going well.

'I've already told you, Mum,' he said. 'It's a matter of life and death.'

Penelope Carter rolled her eyes with the weary expression of someone who has more important things to do than listen to a matter of life and death. 'All you've told me,' she said, as she tied a kitchen apron around her waist, 'is that you have to go to the school sports ground. It's a Saturday, Joe. Surely, it can't be that important?'

Joe took a deep breath and blew it out slowly. 'It's like I said,' he explained, as calmly as he could manage. 'Lucy's running in an important race today and I'm meeting the others so we can cheer her on.'

'Well, there you are then,' said his mother, selecting a knife from the wooden block on the kitchen counter. 'Lucy Yeung spends her whole life running races. She's bound to win; she always does. So why do you have to be there?'

'Because it's what friends do, Mum,' said Joe. 'This race is important for Lucy. If she wins, she'll get to try out for the county athletics squad. I *have* to be there.'

Penelope Carter took a heavy package from the fridge and began to unwrap it. 'As I explained to you, Joseph, I have very important clients coming for dinner tonight and I need you to be here.'

Joe's mother had started a new job, working for an estate agent in the town, which, she explained, meant that she had to 'show houses' to her clients. Joe couldn't imagine why someone had to be shown a house. In his experience, houses generally stayed in one place, and they had addresses so that people could find them easily. Showing people where they were didn't sound like much of a job.

When he pointed this out to his mother, she had become quite annoyed. 'It's not like that, Joe,' she had said, in one of her 'you wouldn't understand' voices. 'The job of an estate agent is very skilled. It's about matching the right sort of people with their ideal property. My clients are people of taste and refinement.'

His mother finished unwrapping the package and studied the contents carefully. Joe looked over her shoulder then recoiled quickly. The package appeared to contain a large blob of slime with tentacles.

'What is *that?*' he said, wrinkling his nose.

'Fresh octopus,' said his mother, as though this was obvious. 'I'm making a seafood stew with a herb salad. It will be lovely.'

Joe stared at the octopus and thought that the last thing it looked was 'lovely'. If this was what people with 'taste and refinement' ate, then he was pretty sure he didn't want to spend an evening with them.

'Are you *sure* you want me there?' he said. 'I mean I wouldn't want to get in the way of that whole "matching people with their ideal property" thing.'

His mother gave him a stern look. 'Oh no you don't, my lad. My clients are extremely important people. Lord and Lady Fitchwitherington are practically related to royalty and tonight they're coming here for dinner and they're bringing their daughter with them. So, I need you to be here.'

Joe sighed. He knew better than to argue with his mother, but there were other ways to get out of the dinner party. If he promised to be back on time, he could always claim later that he'd missed his bus or forgotten the way home.

'Okay, Mum,' he said, putting on his most

sincere smile. 'I'll just pop out for a little while to cheer for Lucy and then I'll be straight back in time for dinner. How's that?'

Penelope Carter fixed her son with the sort of glare that had been known to reduce shop assistants to jelly. 'You'd better be, my lad,' she said, wagging a finger in his direction. 'I want my clients to see that we have a happy and stable home life. So, if you're not back here being happy and stable all evening then you will be spending the rest of half-term confined to your bedroom.'